"You don't owe me anything, Shayla."

The last thing Luke wanted from her was to feel beholden to him. Nor feel a sense of misplaced gratitude for a long-ago act of decency. What he wanted her to feel for him was—

His heart pounded against his ribs. What? What did he want from her?

"Let me do this for you, Luke." She bit her lip. "Please."

He did need her help. With the farm and his mom. So why not let her? And when she gazed at him like that with those big blue eyes of hers…he had a hard time remembering his name, much less refusing her anything. Especially when her offer was so selfless.

Luke stuck out his hand. "Thank you."

"It's a win-win for us both." Shayla shook his hand. "We'll be helping each other. It's what friends do for each other."

But suddenly friendship didn't seem nearly enough…

Lisa Carter and her family make their home in North Carolina. In addition to her Love Inspired novels, she writes romantic suspense. When she isn't writing, Lisa enjoys traveling to romantic locales, teaching writing workshops and researching her next exotic adventure. She has strong opinions on barbecue and ACC basketball. She loves to hear from readers. Connect with Lisa at lisacarterauthor.com.

Books by Lisa Carter

Love Inspired

Visit the Author Profile page at Harlequin.com.

A Safe Place
for Christmas

Lisa Carter

LOVE INSPIRED
INSPIRATIONAL ROMANCE

If you purchased this book without a cover you should be aware
that this book is stolen property. It was reported as "unsold and
destroyed" to the publisher, and neither the author nor the
publisher has received any payment for this "stripped book."

LOVE INSPIRED®
INSPIRATIONAL ROMANCE

PLEASE RECYCLE · THIS PRODUCT IS RECYCLABLE

Recycling programs
for this product may
not exist in your area.

ISBN-13: 978-1-335-56728-4

A Safe Place for Christmas

Copyright © 2021 by Lisa Carter

All rights reserved. No part of this book may be used or reproduced in
any manner whatsoever without written permission except in the case of
brief quotations embodied in critical articles and reviews.

This is a work of fiction. Names, characters, places and incidents are either the
product of the author's imagination or are used fictitiously. Any resemblance
to actual persons, living or dead, businesses, companies, events or locales is
entirely coincidental.

This edition published by arrangement with Harlequin Books S.A.

For questions and comments about the quality of this book, please contact us
at CustomerService@Harlequin.com.

Love Inspired
22 Adelaide St. West, 40th Floor
Toronto, Ontario M5H 4E3, Canada
www.Harlequin.com

Printed in U.S.A.

As every man hath received the gift, even so minister the same one to another, as good stewards of the manifold grace of God.
—*1 Peter* 4:10

To my daughters and husband.

You've been there for me every step
of the journey. And in those final weeks
before deadline, thank you for giving me the
freedom and space to share the gift of words
with Love Inspired readers.

Chapter One

Driving toward the Tennessee state line, Shayla exited off the highway toward the one place she'd found for a time a small measure of happiness. In the small town of Truelove in the Blue Ridge Mountains of North Carolina, she'd made friends. And allowed herself to care for people there.

She should've known the brief interlude of happiness couldn't last. Last spring, her face appeared in the background of a photo in the local newspaper detailing the aftermath of the devastating tornado that hit the mountain hamlet. She'd had no choice but to run again.

At the top of the exit ramp, she contemplated the sign indicating Truelove to the left. Her mouth twisted. *True love.* Like that actually existed. Or maybe just not for her.

She couldn't go back there. Not after quitting her job at the Mason Jar Café, leaving her boss and friend, Kara, understaffed. She'd burned her bridges. No going back to Truelove.

Instead, she veered right. It was the longer way, the less-traveled path to Tennessee. But she'd get there just the same.

Her ex-boyfriend, Wall, was less likely to intercept her on these country roads. Perhaps the photo had been a false alarm. In the intervening months since she'd left Truelove, his cronies hadn't found her. But yesterday, when she'd learned he'd been released on a technicality, she realized it was time to move again.

She focused on the isolated secondary road. The yellow lines on the pavement wound higher and higher, like stripes on a candy cane. She topped the mountain range and began a slow descent.

The car sputtered.

"No…" She strangled the wheel. "Don't quit on me now. Please…"

With one final, convulsive hiccup, the engine died.

This couldn't be happening to her. Not now, when she was so desperate to put as many miles as she could between herself and danger.

She glanced in the rearview mirror at the deserted road behind her. A reflex. Always looking over her shoulder. Always afraid he'd find her. Always on the run.

What should she do? Undoing her seat belt, she

angled around to check on her baby, strapped into his car seat in the back. Thankfully, Jeremiah was still at the age where he slept more than he was awake. Would it be better to stay in the vehicle and hope for a passerby? Or should she get out and start walking?

On this cold, late-November afternoon, the heat from the car had already begun to dissipate. Her breath fogged. That was enough to make her decision.

It could be hours before another vehicle happened along the remote stretch of road. Jeremiah wouldn't survive in these temperatures. And suppose Wall found them? They'd be sitting ducks.

She opened the door and got out. Fallen brown leaves carpeted the shoulder of the road, crunching under her brown ankle boots. Careful not to wake her infant son, she eased open the rear door.

Taking off her coat, she draped the baby sling around her neck and let it hang next to her sweater. Donning her coat once more, she leaned into the back seat, putting her knee into the upholstery. After unbuckling Jeremiah, she positioned him inside the wrap.

She bundled him inside her oversize winter coat, buttoning it around him. Keeping him snuggled against her warmth. Leaving his nose and mouth exposed so he could breathe freely.

Would he be warm enough? She pressed her

lips to the soft, knitted wool cap on his small head. "I'm sorry, baby. So sorry."

Sorry she'd made so many terrible choices. Including becoming involved with his father, Wall Phillips. Sorry she'd made a complete mess out of not only her life, but her baby's, as well.

Jeremiah stirred. Her heart leaped. But his cheek resting against her chest, he nestled and settled without waking.

She scanned the road from left to right. The colorful autumn display for which the region was renowned had given way to winter-barren trees, lifting their skeletal arms to the milky sunshine in a gray sky. Not many hours of daylight left.

Here in the Blue Ridge, once the sun dropped behind the range of mountains, the light would go out like a match extinguished.

No evidence of civilization in either direction. Nothing but forest as far as she could see on both sides of the road.

"Which way should I choose, God?" she whispered in a puff of breath.

A question she should've asked at the exit ramp.

But in this back-of-beyond section of North Carolina, the silence was broken only by her son's soft breathing and the gentle sound of falling leaves.

Her father would've laughed to hear her talk to God. He'd turned his back on God after her mama ran away to Nashville when Shayla was a little girl.

One arm holding her baby against herself, she pulled out the backpack that contained all of their worldly goods. She slipped her arms through the straps. She didn't bother to lock the car. If someone wanted to steal this rusted heap of junk, they could have it.

She wasn't sure where she was. When night fell, the temperatures would plunge. If she didn't find shelter, she and Jeremiah would die. She swallowed the sob rising in her throat.

Eyes stinging from the cold, she blinked the tears away. She didn't have to imagine what her father would say. *Dry it up before I give you something to cry about.* She'd found out the hard way that unlike her father, Wall didn't just threaten. He preferred to use his fists.

But no more. She lifted her chin. Whatever it took, whatever she had to do, she'd make sure Jeremiah's life was better.

Perhaps if she hiked the eight miles into Truelove, someone could give her a lift to the county seat. She had enough money for a bus ticket over the mountains. Surely the bus company wouldn't charge her for Jeremiah. She'd hold him in her lap the entire journey.

The irony of riding the bus to Tennessee like her mom had twenty years ago didn't escape Shayla. But to keep Jeremiah safe, she'd do what she had to. Such a shame her mother hadn't thought the same. But she wasn't like her irresponsible mother. She'd die before leaving her child behind.

She took a step forward, then another—each a step closer to following her dream. Toward freedom. Toward safety. Toward finding home.

Getting over the state line was crucial. Once there, Wall couldn't touch her. The conditions of the ongoing case against him would prevent him from traveling out of state and at long last, she'd be safe.

She'd been walking about five minutes when she detected the sound of a vehicle coming up hard and fast on the road. She froze. Her heart pounded.

Was it him? How had Wall found her so quickly? Sudden panic descended. She quickened her pace, which was foolish. She'd never outrun him, especially not carrying Jeremiah in her arms. Fear descended like a smothering mantle.

Oh, God, please protect us.

Topping the ridge on the mountain road in his blue Chevy truck, Luke Morgan slowed at a flicker of orange in the curve ahead.

The bright orange scarf belonged to a slight figure. A woman, clad in jeans and bundled in a large, dark overcoat, walked alone on the road. At the realization, he hit the brakes. The truck skidded. The rear end fishtailed. Her eyes appeared impossibly large and frightened.

Don't let me hit her, God.

Luke tightened his grip on the wheel. He fought to keep the truck from veering off the pavement. Coming off the mountain, a fierce headwind threatened to sweep everything to the valley floor below. Mere yards from the petite woman, his vehicle shuddered to a stop.

Chest heaving, his gaze darted from the precarious edge where the shoulder dropped off to nothingness to the solid granite mountain wall on the other side. His heart raced. That had been close. Too close.

Her hair stuffed underneath a black knit cap and her hands stuffed in the pockets of her coat, she gaped at him through the windshield. What was she doing out here by herself?

With the engine rumbling, he lowered the window and poked out his head. "Ma'am? Can I help you? Is everything all right?"

A shadow passed over her face. Terror flashed in her eyes before a spark of recognition took its place. In the same split second, he remembered her, too.

"Shayla? Shayla Coggins?"

Her blue eyes flitted to the signage on his truck. "Morgan Farm. Christmas trees, right?"

The motor idled. "It's Luke."

He peered through the windshield at the road. He didn't see a vehicle. How had she gotten here?

What was she doing out here alone? "Did you have car trouble?"

She gestured behind her. "It quit on me."

"You're a waitress at the Mason Jar Café."

A rosy color matching the tip of her nose tinted her cheeks. "I used to be." She buried her chin in the orange scarf at her throat.

Luke tried to recall the last time he'd seen Shayla. Maybe last spring? And then she hadn't been around anymore. But in the aftermath of the tornado, he'd been caught up in rebuilding the town.

He felt a vague sense of guilt he hadn't noticed her absence. Somebody should've paid attention. It wasn't right a person could vanish so easily and no one had cared enough to investigate.

But in the spring, he'd also been absorbed in the ongoing, increasingly futile effort to save the tree farm. Yet one more example of how badly he'd failed not only his late father, but his mom and sisters, too. He'd be the one who lost the Morgan heritage. The six-generation family farm.

He glanced at her wind-scrubbed face. Deep in the mountains with dusk falling, this wasn't the safest place for a person to be walking. There was nothing between Truelove and the Tennessee state line, except scattered farms, the national forest and plunging gorges.

"Can I give you a ride? Let me take you home."

"No." Her face clouded. "Not there."

Too late he remembered she'd lived in one of the more remote hollers across the river. A disreputable trailer park, populated largely by people who skated the thin line of the law.

Not much of a place to call home.

"There's no need to trouble yourself." She turned away from the window. "I can manage. Thank you, though."

As small as she was, her voice had a low alto quality to it. Reminding him of a deep pool at the basin of a waterfall. A knot tightened in the pit of his belly.

"Wait, Shayla... Where are you headed?"

They'd gone to the same county high school. She was younger than Luke by a few years. But her eyes... Her eyes were old.

Her expression became wary. "I—I haven't decided yet." Her long, dark lashes swept against her pale skin, and she quickly veiled her gaze.

Luke wasn't sure how he knew she wasn't telling him the truth, but he did. She knew perfectly well where she was headed, and didn't trust him enough to share the information.

He had a suspicion if he counted the number of people Shayla Coggins trusted, he wouldn't even use all the fingers on one hand.

"My friend Zach owns the auto repair shop in Truelove." Luke picked his phone off the console.

"How about I give him a call? He can tow your car and determine the problem."

She shook her head. "Some things can't be fixed." Tendrils of blond hair escaped her black cap.

He had the feeling she was talking about more than her vehicle.

"I can't pay him for a tow." She jutted her chin. "Or to fix my car." Her eyes blazed.

And his heart did a quick staccato step. Why had he never noticed the lovely shade of her eyes? A startling blue, as clear and vibrant as a mountain-crisp autumn sky.

Her lips thinned. "I don't take charity."

"Of course not. But it's getting dark, Shayla. There's snow forecast to sweep over the mountains tonight. I can't leave you standing out here."

At that moment, a tiny snowflake drifted out of the sky, floated downward and stuck to the windshield. Those fabulous eyes of hers flickered.

"Please get in the truck. We'll figure something out." He raised his hands to shoulder height. "I promise you, I'm not a serial killer."

A smile flitted across her lips, so brief as to nearly make him believe he'd imagined it.

"I know you're not." She wrapped her arms around herself. "Unlike the others, you were always kind to me."

They'd gone to a small high school. Tainted by

the stain of her jailbird father and brothers, she'd been ostracized by most of her peers. He should've made more of an effort to make sure she was okay.

But the one year of school they'd shared had been the year his father, struggling with ALS, had taken a downward turn. As a senior, Luke had more on his mind than the painfully thin little freshman. However, it seemed God had given him another chance to be a man who would've made his father proud.

"My mom would kill me if I didn't invite you to dinner. Mountain hospitality demands it. You'd be doing me a favor." He flashed her a smile. "Please don't let my mother kill me, Shayla."

Somewhere on the road behind him, he heard a car charging over the pass. Her expression changed. Something akin to panic streaked across her features. Shivering, she yanked open the door and hopped inside the cab.

"Thanks for the invite." She slammed the door shut. "Best not keep her waiting."

Okay... He put the truck in motion. "Buckle up."

She stretched the belt wide before clicking it into the receptacle between them. Over the next few minutes, he couldn't help but notice how often she glanced in the side mirror. And she clutched the door handle poised for flight.

A vehicle edged up behind them. The driver

of the SUV put on his blinker to pass and came alongside. She sank down into the seat.

Luke cut his eyes at her. "Is something wrong?"

The SUV blew past them.

She sat up and peered through the windshield. "I'm—"

A mewling cry erupted, jolting him.

"What's that?"

Shayla's eyes jerked from the red taillights of the vehicle disappearing around the next hairpin curve to him. The orange scarf at the base of her throat rippled. Out of its confines, a tiny fist flailed.

He gasped. "Is that a baby?"

Shayla's arms went around her coat.

He slowed, veered off onto one of the mountain lookouts and hit the brakes.

She rocked the child hidden underneath her coat. "Shh…shh…"

"You have a baby?"

Unbuttoning her coat, she drew out a tiny infant, clasped close to her body in a baby sling thingy. The orange scarf was actually the baby's knitted wool cap.

The high-pitched cries intensified. His heart hammered.

Her family's reputation flashed through his mind. Drug dealing. Grand theft auto. What had he gotten himself involved in with Shayla?

He clenched his jaw. "Who does that baby belong to?"

She gave him a cool stare. "The baby belongs to me."

"But when you worked at the Mason Jar..."

She jiggled the crying baby in her arms. "I was already pregnant when I worked at the café."

Had café owner Kara MacKenzie known? Had the entire town? Was he the only clueless one?

Last spring, Shayla hadn't appeared to be expecting. But then, she'd always been so thin and petite. His gaze cut to her ringless finger. A glance that, unfortunately, she noticed.

"Not that it's any of your business." Her mouth pulled downward. "But I'm not, nor have I ever been, married."

He flushed. He hadn't remembered the soft-spoken waitress being so...so belligerent. She'd always struck him as shy. Like him. But perhaps circumstances had forced her to become more assertive.

The baby continued to wail. Luke rubbed his forehead. She brushed her lips across its tiny head, trying in vain to comfort the child.

Had he made a mistake in inviting her to the farm? He lifted his Morgan Farm ball cap off his head and resettled it. Face scrunched and angry, the thrashing infant appeared apoplectic.

Luke was not good with babies. "Can't you get it to stop crying already?"

"*It* happens to be my son, Jeremiah," she hissed. "And he's hungry."

Luke went red. "Oh."

"I recognize where I am now. The Apple Valley Orchard isn't far. I'll walk the rest of the way," she rasped. "No need for you to get stuck with us…" She laid her hand on the latch.

For a second, he feared she might hurl herself from the truck. "Shayla, don't go." He touched her coat sleeve. "I didn't mean to offend you. The baby just surprised me."

Lips tightening, her eyes flew to his hand and then to his face. "I'll be fine… I always am, Mr. Morgan."

He very much doubted the truth of that.

"It's Luke," he growled.

He scrubbed his face with his hand. "Supper first. And then I'll drop you off wherever you want to go."

She looked at him a long moment. For reasons he didn't entirely understand, he found himself holding his breath, awaiting her answer.

"All right," she said finally. "But the last bus leaves the county terminal at nine tonight, and I need to be on it."

His stomach tightening, Luke held her gaze

a moment longer. Because the prospect of her leaving Truelove filled him with an inexplicable dismay.

Chapter Two

Shayla turned away from him. "While we're stopped, I should feed him. He won't stop crying until I do."

Luke reddened. "Sure. Go ahead."

She reached into the backpack in the foot of the cab. For modesty's sake, she placed a blanket over the baby. She looked at Luke, but he'd averted his face. A gentleman, much as she remembered.

After feeding Jeremiah, she placed him snugly inside the sling. "Sorry for the delay." Closing his eyes, Jeremiah nestled against her and fell asleep again. She refastened the seat belt around them. "We're ready now."

Cheeks flushed, Luke put the truck into motion. He kept his gaze fastened on the road, which gave her the chance to get her first real look at him.

The width of his broad shoulders underneath the tan Carhartt jacket indicated the boy she'd known in high school had grown into a man. But he still possessed the boy-next-door good looks she recalled. A five-o'clock shadow stubbled his strong jawline. And the lines at the corners of his chocolate-brown eyes hadn't been there before. Laugh lines or sorrow?

For his sake, she hoped the former. He'd been a quiet sort of boy. Yet his solemn features also bore the stamp of a maturity she sensed had not been easily won.

Perhaps feeling her scrutiny, he looked at her. Caught out, she blushed.

She focused on the passing scenery. "Maybe you should call to let your folks know you're bringing us for supper."

"There's always plenty. And it's only my mom and sisters and me." His voice deepened. "My father died the summer I graduated."

"Oh, I'm sorry." She angled toward him. "You were headed to…" She cast her mind back. "To the university. You were a writer. The editor of the school newspaper, right?"

"Never made it to college." His face, if possible, became even more stoic. "After Dad died, I was needed here."

"Do you still write?"

"No." His handsome mouth thinned. "I put aside those foolish dreams a long time ago."

"Dreams aren't foolish." She brushed her cheek against the soft wool of Jeremiah's cap.

"Life happens." He flicked a look her way. "I'm guessing you know that better than anyone. Of necessity, I became a Christmas tree farmer. And you, a mother."

"That isn't the sum total of who we are, though." She wrapped her arms around her son. "Aren't we allowed to reach for more?"

"When my father died, I had to grow up fast. And shoulder the responsibilities that came with my new reality." He gripped the wheel. "You, too. Can I ask, where's the kid's dad?"

She took a quick look out the side mirror. But the truck was the only vehicle on the isolated mountain road. It was her sense of responsibility for her son that had sent her scrambling for safety.

"His biological father won't be in our lives." If she had her way, Wall Phillips would never get his hands on her innocent child.

She glanced at the mirror once more. When her gaze returned, she found Luke studying her. His eyebrows furrowed. She dropped her chin.

It hurt to contemplate what he must think of her. Another mountain statistic. Young, unmarried and poor with a baby to raise. Probably wondering if she even knew the identity of Jeremiah's father.

Yet coming from such an upstanding, salt-of-the-earth family, Luke would have no understanding of what her life had truly been like. And somehow his low opinion bothered her more than it should.

"You were on your way home from Truelove?"

"I was getting the tree lot ready on the town square for opening day on Friday."

"Friday?"

He gave her a funny look. "The day after Thanksgiving. It's the first day of the Christmas tree season."

"Thanksgiving is this week?" She blinked. "I— I'd forgotten."

It was not a holiday celebrated in her family. *Give thanks for what?* her father would've said. But in the shelter where she'd found a temporary refuge after leaving Truelove, there'd been a Bible in the nightstand by her bed. During the last month of her pregnancy, she'd read it daily.

She nuzzled her lips against her son's cap. Despite the circumstances of his conception and birth, she was thankful for Jeremiah. He was perhaps the only person who'd ever truly loved her. And she was amazed and humbled by the love she felt for him.

Rattling along the winding road, Luke drove the classic Chevy deeper and higher into the hardwood forests of the Blue Ridge. Due to her family's obsession with cars, she knew more than her fair share about automotive vehicles. Snowflakes continued to drift lazily from the sky. Dusting the pavement, the precipitation started to stick to the winter-brown grass on the shoulder of the road.

At the sign for the Morgan Farm, he veered off the rural road onto a long, graveled driveway. He steered through a grove of trees. Between standing rows of evergreens, she caught her first glimpse of the Morgan family homestead.

The green-tin-roofed two-story white farmhouse with a wraparound porch and stone chimney crowned the top of a knoll. Lights shone from nearly every window.

Behind the house lay a barn and a white outbuilding. Rolling acres of Christmas trees surrounded the entire complex on three sides. On the horizon, the Blue Ridge Mountains undulated like the folds of a fan, a smoky purple-blue in color, which the region derived its name from.

A small car was parked beside the house. He punched a remote control sensor fastened to the visor. The garage door opened. He pulled into the double bay beside a large SUV.

"Hold on a sec." He threw open the door and got out. "Let me carry your bag."

Luke rounded the engine and offered his hand as she climbed out of the truck. His hand was warm, weathered from work, and strong. Sparks ignited along her skin.

Her breath hitched. His brows arched. But as

soon as her boots touched the concrete, he let go of her hand, the spark evaporating as quickly as it came.

Shouldering her bag, he mounted several wooden steps to a door connected to the house. She followed on his heels. He pushed through into the kitchen.

"I waited dinner for you, Luke." At the stove, an attractive, trim brunette in her midfifties stirred something simmering in a large Dutch oven. "Did you get delayed in town?"

He set the backpack on the floor. "Not exactly."

Looking up, his mother spotted Shayla hovering uncertainly on the threshold. "Oh. Hi." Her gaze darted to her son.

"Mom, this is Shayla. Her car broke down on the road." He shuffled his feet. "I invited her to dinner. Then I'm going to run her over to the bus station to catch the overnight to Tennessee."

Smiling, his mother offered her hand. "I'm Emily Morgan. I'm glad you could join us."

"Is Luke finally home?" someone shouted from upstairs.

"I'm starving," another voice moaned.

Skipping down the stairs, two young women popped into the cozy kitchen. Catching sight of Shayla, they exchanged curious glances.

"My sisters, Caroline and Krista." He stuffed his hands in his pockets. "This is Shayla."

Slim, with straight brown hair and brown eyes, Caroline looked like her mom. "There was a Shayla who used to waitress at the café." Somehow Luke's twentyish sister managed to make jeans and the gray sweatshirt with the college logo seem elegant. "Shayla Coggins?"

Caroline would have been several grades behind her at school, a pretty girl who'd blossomed into a lovely young woman.

Profoundly conscious of the spit-up on the collar of her coat and the extra inches around her middle, Shayla suddenly felt grubby. "Yes, that's me."

Deciding now might be a good time to wake up, Jeremiah arched his back like a cat, creating a small bulging wave under her coat.

In her late teens, Luke's youngest sibling leaned forward. "Is that a baby?" Brown eyes sparkling, Krista grinned. "You have a baby under there, don't you? How fun."

Jeremiah squirmed. Shayla's arms went around him. His days in the baby wrap were numbered. When awake, he no longer wanted to be confined or swaddled as much as he had in the first months of his life.

Unbuttoning her coat, she drew her baby out of the sling. "This is Jeremiah."

"Ooh." Hands clasped under her chin, Krista bounced in her stocking feet. "He's so cute. Isn't he, Mom?"

In contrast to her sister, Krista was shorter, more like Shayla. But unlike Shayla's blond locks, Krista's loose, brown curls cascaded down her back. All three women crowded around her.

Emily Morgan smiled. "Absolutely adorable. How old is he?"

Shayla rocked Jeremiah. "He's five-and-a-half months old."

Luke's mom held out her arms. "Would he let me take him?"

"I—I don't know." Supporting his head, she propped the baby against her shoulder. "He's not used to strangers."

Emily gave her a wistful smile. "It's been so long since I held a little one. I could hold him while you eat dinner."

"Oh, I wouldn't want to impose."

Emily cradled Jeremiah's wispy blond head in her palm. "It would be my pleasure. Caroline," she called over her shoulder. "Dish out the stew. Krista, pour the tea. Luke, wash your hands, and let's sit down."

Jeremiah was going to have to get used to others caring for him. And so was she. Once she got a job in Nashville, she'd have no choice but to hand him over to strangers every day at a day care.

But that didn't make it any easier now. Not wanting to appear rude, yet feeling great reluctance, she handed Jeremiah off to Mrs. Morgan.

How quickly she'd come to think of him as an extension of herself.

Her arms feeling strangely empty, she sat next to Krista. Across the farmhouse table, Caroline took the opposite chair. Luke seated himself at one end. Holding Jeremiah in her arms, Emily sat down at the other end of the table.

"But, Mrs. Morgan..." Shayla started to rise. "You won't get to eat."

Emily motioned her back. "We'll take turns."

Luke bowed his head. Shayla did the same. Something else she'd learned at the shelter—the giving of thanks, saying grace for meals.

Everyone dug into the delicious chicken stew. She couldn't remember the last time she'd been able to eat an entire meal without stopping to tend to her baby. She stayed quiet, letting the flow of conversation hum around her.

Her family hadn't been the sort that did family dinners. She was grateful the Morgans didn't ask her a bunch of awkward questions.

As she ate, she took a quick survey of her surroundings. The Morgan house was a real home, the kind she so desperately wanted Jeremiah to know. But who was she kidding? Who'd ever want to marry her, a single mom with a kid?

Despite the blustery wind outside, the kitchen was cozy and cheerful. The dining chairs were painted either a rooster red, a sage green or a buttery yellow. They matched the large, oval braided rug underneath the table, covering the pinewood floor.

A log burned inside the bricked hearth of the double-sided fireplace, providing warmth to the kitchen and, on the other side, to the family room outfitted with comfortable furniture.

Bubbly Krista made a joke. Everyone laughed. What would it have been like to grow up in a house like this? She hoped Luke's sisters appreciated how blessed they were.

How different would her life have been if she'd been born to a family like the Morgans? Extremely different because she would have made very different choices.

Jeremiah made cooing noises. His big, blue eyes were riveted on Emily Morgan. His face had been taken over by a big smile, and his arms and legs waved in the air.

Yet, if she'd been part of a family like the Morgans, Jeremiah probably would've never existed. Despite the pain and heartache she'd endured since falling into Wall's unscrupulous clutches, she couldn't wish for Jeremiah to never have been born. She loved him too much.

Only gradually did she realize that while the Morgan women carried the conversation at the dinner table, Luke remained as silent as Shayla.

Eventually, his silence penetrated his family's happy chatter.

His mother handed Jeremiah to Caroline. "Any trouble setting up the tree lot on the square?" She picked up her fork. "I assume the final wholesale order went out this afternoon."

Luke straightened. "It did. The lot at the square is good to go, too."

Krista got up from the table and returned with a tea pitcher. "Shayla?"

She shook her head. "No, thanks."

Krista refilled Luke's glass. "Ready for Open House on Friday, big bro?"

He took a sip and set the glass on the table. "I was going over the checklist in my head."

"My brother is a workaholic." Rolling her eyes, Caroline held Jeremiah in her arms. "He doesn't know the meaning of the word *relax*."

Luke frowned. "I've got too much to do and too little time to do it. This season is make-or-break for the farm."

Krista hugged the tea pitcher. "Are we going to have to sell the house, Mom?"

His mother pushed away her plate.

Caroline's eyes widened. "He's exaggerating, isn't he?"

He raked his hand through his light brown hair. "Forget I said anything. It'll be fine. I'll make sure of it."

Krista gave him a quick hug. "Of course you will." She smiled at Shayla. "Luke can fix anything. He's never let us down before and he won't now."

Caroline perked. "He'll find a way. He always does."

Luke's gaze dropped to the table. "No need for y'all to worry."

He appeared exhausted and very alone at the head of the table. Nearly as alone as she'd felt most of her life.

She looked at his sisters, cuddling Jeremiah, and at his mother, finishing her dinner. Why should they worry? Not when they had Luke to worry for them. But who, she wondered, feeling mildly outraged on his behalf, worried about him?

Abruptly she pushed back her chair. Worrying about Luke Morgan was not her job. She had worries enough with Jeremiah and their current situation.

"Thank you so much for the wonderful meal, Mrs. Morgan." She started scraping plates. "I insist on doing the dishes."

Krista jumped up. "You're our guest."

"I don't want to lose my waitress skills." She made a bundle of silverware. "If y'all wouldn't mind keeping Jeremiah company for a little while…"

Holding Jeremiah, Caroline rose from the

table. "I don't mind entertaining this precious little buddy."

Krista planted her hands on her hips. "When am I going to get my turn with the snuggle bunny?"

Shayla laughed. "Snuggle bunny? I'll have to remember that."

It was good for Jeremiah to have someone else to play with. Caroline and Krista were sweet to take an interest in him.

"You'll both get a turn." Their mother motioned toward the living room. "Sit on the couch with him."

Luke put his hand on her shoulder. "I'll help Shayla in the kitchen."

Emily's forehead creased. "But you've been loading trees all day. You must be dead on your feet."

"You and the girls have been making wreaths all day." He hugged her. "Enjoy yourself for once. I know how you love babies. We'll clear up dinner before I run Shayla to the bus station."

The bus station. Oh, yeah. That. She'd enjoyed his family so much she'd almost forgotten she was merely passing through. If only she didn't have to leave. She could stay here forever.

Not possible, of course. But no harm in dreaming. For most of her life, dreams had been her best and only companion.

At the sink, she stood shoulder to shoulder with

Luke. They made an efficient team. She did the washing, and he did the drying. He wasn't much for small talk, which was okay by her.

She handed him a glass.

Catching her eye, he flushed and looked away. "I'm sorry."

She rested her hip against the counter. "About what?"

"For not being a great conversationalist." He dried the glass. "My sisters complain I don't know how to talk about anything other than the farm and restoring Chevys from the 1950s."

She rinsed another glass. "Talking is way over-rated."

Wall had been ridiculously charming, and she'd fallen for it. Hook, line and sinker.

"I happen to be interested in your farm *and* in vintage trucks." She passed another glass to him. "It's not the volume of words that count, but their sincerity."

He put down the glass. "You think I'm sincere?"

"And honest."

He grimaced. "My sisters would probably say both are girl-speak for boring."

"You're not boring." Luke Morgan was vastly underappreciated by his sisters. "If my brothers had an ounce of the work ethic you do…" She cut off her train of thought.

It was best not to bring her family into it. No

doubt everyone in the county, including Luke, knew about her brothers.

He set the glass in the cabinet above the drainer. "Are you headed to your brothers in Tennessee?"

"No." As always when she talked about her family, she felt the telltale red flush creeping up her chest and across her neck. "At present, they're enjoying the hospitality of the North Carolina Department of Correction."

"I'm sorry." He dried a plate. "What about your dad?"

Her heart thumped. "My father and brothers have made bad choices." Pulling the lever on the faucet, she rinsed a handful of silverware. "I'm trying to make better ones."

A baby chuckle gurgled from the living room. She cut her eyes to Luke. "Better late than never, right?"

"Do you have a job waiting for you in Tennessee?"

She shook her head.

"Any family or friends there?"

The Cogginses didn't have friends. Not any on the right side of the law. As for family? They either ended up in jail or died young.

Ducking her head, she cleaned a plate. "We'll be fine." When he didn't respond, she stole a look at him.

"You know what's best, I suppose."

She felt a vague sense of disappointment he hadn't tried harder to get her to reconsider. But not wishing to be saddled with her, he'd probably be glad to see the back of them, and she couldn't blame him.

Pulling out the sink plug, she watched the water spiral down the black hole of the drain. An image not unlike her future. A lump unexpectedly formed in her throat.

The enormity of what lay ahead overwhelmed her. The all-night bus ride. Finding a cheap place to stay. Getting a job. Placing Jeremiah in day care. The uphill struggle.

Gripping the porcelain edge of the sink, she blinked back tears. She was so tired of running. So tired of being alone. *Oh, God. Help me.*

Luke spread the drying cloth over the drainer. "I guess we should get on the road now."

She pushed away from the sink. "I—I guess so."

He stared into her face. "Hey, are you all right?"

She swiped at her cheeks. "I should check Jeremiah's diaper first." Heading for the living room, she hoped her eyes weren't too red and her face didn't betray how low she felt.

Or how terribly afraid she was of the unknown.

Luke followed Shayla into the living room. His sisters sat on the red leather couch on either side of his mom, who held the infant on her lap.

His mother smiled at him. "Would you like to hold Jeremiah?"

Luke backed toward the recliner. "No, thanks. I'm good."

As was his habit, he checked the weather forecast on his phone. Over the mountains, east Tennessee had already gotten hit with a ton of snow.

He didn't get the fascination with babies. He'd been in kindergarten when Caroline was born, too busy with school and friends to care about his new, tiny sibling. By the time Krista was born, he was old enough to be embarrassed his mom was pregnant again.

Shayla held out her arms for her baby. "I should check his diaper before we go."

Krista scrambled off the couch. "So soon? But you just got here."

His mom handed the baby to Shayla. "Jeremiah is such a sweetheart."

"Thank you." She gathered her son close. "This has been so nice, sharing dinner with you. But we've got a bus to catch."

He couldn't deny she did look a picture. A right nice picture. Standing there with the baby in her arms, her wavy blond hair framed her heart-shaped face.

Kind of how he envisioned the rest of his life playing out eventually, with a wife and a couple of kids. Key word—*eventually*. No rush.

After his father's premature death, he'd had his hands full keeping the farm solvent. And with his sisters' college expenses adding to the farm's debt, he was in no hurry to find a wife. His buddies had taken the plunge years ago. Last man standing, he'd get around to it.

Once the farm got back on track financially, he'd give the idea of a wife serious thought. He liked to take his time. To properly evaluate a situation from every angle before making a decision.

He needed somebody easygoing, who understood the rigors of being a farmer's wife. Cheerful, hardworking, no drama.

Luke flicked a glance at the petite blonde. He sensed major drama with Shayla. *Good thing she was leaving.* So why, then, did his heart skip a beat at the notion of her walking out the door? Out of his life? And he was having a hard time not gazing into her startling blue eyes.

It irritated him to no end why it even mattered.

Krista took Shayla upstairs to change the baby in the spare room. A few minutes later, they came downstairs again. Krista held Jeremiah while Shayla reorganized the backpack.

She had a hard time sitting still, he'd noticed. Antsy. Anxious to be off. Like a caged bird.

With the sleeping baby tucked against her, Krista peered out the window into the night. "The snow is coming down pretty hard. Are you sure you want Jeremiah out in this, Shayla?"

Caroline gave them a brilliant smile. "Stay the night. One of us can run you to the station tomorrow morning."

His mother leaned forward on the sofa. "You and Jeremiah must be exhausted from traveling today. Get a good night's sleep in our guest bedroom. And take the scheduled morning departure. You'll be well rested, and Jeremiah will probably cope better, too."

Shayla peered out the window at the falling snow. "I appreciate the invitation, but I have to get on the bus tonight."

Had to? Why, when she'd admitted no one, not even a job, awaited her in Nashville? What was the urgency?

Something seemed off about her situation. Was it just stubbornness or something else?

"I'm sorry to ask you to drive us in this weather." She looked at him. "With conditions deteriorating, is it still possible?"

He shrugged into his coat. "It's liable to take longer to reach the bus station. We should leave now."

Caroline planted a quick kiss on Jeremiah's chubby cheeks. "Do you have your bus ticket?"

Shaking her head, Shayla pulled on her overcoat.

Caroline positioned the orange cap on Jeremiah's head. "You should purchase it online."

Lips tight, Shayla zipped the backpack. "I don't have a cell phone."

Caroline blinked at her. "You don't have a cell phone?"

He tossed his sister an annoyed look. Caroline had a kind heart, but too often she was simply clueless. She'd spent the last few years at the university, leading a carefree coed existence.

Which was entirely his fault. After Dad died, he made sure neither of his sisters wanted for anything. Sheltering them from the sort of harsh realities he imagined Shayla had faced most of her life.

Shayla slipped her arms through the straps of the backpack. "I left my phone in Durham."

"Oh, honey. How terrible." His mother blew out a breath. "And when you discovered you'd accidentally left your phone, you were probably too far away to turn around."

Stuffing tendrils of her hair under the wool hat, Shayla dropped her gaze. Something in her expression made him wonder if her cell had been left behind accidentally or on purpose.

Caroline spread the baby's blanket on the couch. "That's a long way to drive with Jeremiah and no phone."

Krista laid the baby on the blanket. "Suppose something had happened?" Luke's sisters bundled the infant inside the soft blue fleece. His mom picked him up.

"Nothing happened." Shayla jutted her chin. "Until the car died."

Krista picked her phone off the coffee table. "But prepurchasing tickets now could save time so you won't miss the bus." She typed into the search engine and scrolled. "I'll just need your credit card."

"I—I don't…" Shayla bit her lip. "I'll buy the ticket at the station."

His heart jerked. She didn't have a credit card, did she? Did she even have enough money for the bus? His family exchanged anxious glances.

"Let me start the truck and get the cab warm for the baby." He moved toward the kitchen. "I'll be back in a sec."

Inside the garage, he cranked the motor and notched up the heat. Raising the garage door, he surveyed the rapidly descending snow outside and shook his head.

Returning to the house, he found everyone in the kitchen waiting for him.

She took the baby from his mother. "Again, thank you so much for your hospitality."

"It was our pleasure, sweetie." His mom hugged her. "Please let us know when you and Jeremiah arrive. Maybe you could borrow a phone to make the call. I'll be praying for you."

His sisters rushed forward to say their good-byes. Shayla's eyes shimmered as she tore herself away. He leaped forward to open the door. At the blast of frigid air, she shivered, but setting her face forward, she ventured out.

Luke turned toward his mother. "Should I offer to buy her ticket? Not that I'm exactly rolling in money these days, either."

His mom patted his arm. "Do what you can to make sure they get on the bus okay. And be careful driving home."

Luke shut the door behind him. Inside the cab, Shayla had placed the baby in the wrap thing once more. It worried him the child had no proper car seat for the ride over the mountains. Especially in these conditions.

He was feeling increasingly uneasy about her setting off on a journey over the mountains in a snowstorm with an infant, no cell phone and very little cash.

After getting into the truck, he fisted his hands around the steering wheel. This was a mistake. He felt almost physically ill at the prospect of leaving her at the bus station.

"What's wrong?" Her lovely brow wrinkled.

Here goes nothing.

Luke braced for the fallout. "I've got money— not much, but enough for the bus and a few nights in a motel once you reach Nashville."

Those beautiful eyes of hers clouded.

"Before you say no…" He held up his hand.

"Think of it as a loan. You can repay me after you get your first paycheck. With interest, if it makes you feel better about accepting it."

She chewed her lip. "Like at the Burger Depot."

He scrunched his brow. "I'm sorry. What?"

"In high school."

Their eyes locked, and he found himself unable—unwilling—to tear his gaze away.

"You really don't remember, Luke?"

He was definitely missing something.

"Of course you wouldn't." She sighed. "That's just who you are." She gave him a small, sad smile. "And yet once again, I seem to find myself in desperate need of your financial assistance."

He had no idea what she was talking about.

"But this time…" She wagged her finger. "Write down your address, and I'll pay you back. With interest."

He stuck out his hand. "Deal?"

"Deal." She shook his hand. He felt a zing tingle on his skin. "Oh." She rubbed her fingers on her jeans. "Static electricity."

He swallowed, hard. *Yeah. Sure. What else could it be, right?*

Best to not touch her again. His stomach tanked, though he couldn't think why. Maybe dinner hadn't agreed with him.

He glanced over his shoulder to reverse out of the garage.

"Wait! Luke! Wait!"

He whipped around. Running down the steps into the garage, Krista raised her cell phone. "Stop!"

He lowered the window. "We're kinda in a hurry here, Kris."

"I'm so glad I caught you."

He made a face. This had better not be about stopping by the store on the way home. This definitely wasn't a night to linger in the elements.

"I was on the bus station website." She waved the phone in his face. "Due to whiteout conditions and snow accumulations, the pass over the mountains to Tennessee has been closed. The bus route has been canceled, and the terminal shut down."

Shayla groaned. "For how long?"

Krista rolled through the alert on her screen. "Until the Department of Transportation can get a crew up there."

"But with Thanksgiving the day after tomorrow…" Shayla cradled her baby. "How soon do you think they'll have the highway clear?"

Shutting off the engine, he grinned at Shayla. "Looks like you're stuck with us until at least Monday."

And weirdly, the knot in his gut eased.

Chapter Three

The next morning, Shayla awoke in the guest bedroom. Working at the Mason Jar Café last spring, she'd gotten into the habit of waking early. Which proved to be excellent training for becoming Jeremiah's mom. He liked to wake with the first rays of the sun.

But she shouldn't complain. He was already sleeping through the night. Such a good, sweet baby.

A bright, white light shone around the edge of the curtains. Propping herself up on her elbow, she peered over the edge of the mattress at her son in the small crib Emily Morgan had unearthed from the attic.

Jeremiah lay quietly on his back, tiny arms and legs waving.

"Good job letting Mommy enjoy a few extra winks of sleep," she whispered.

At the sound of her voice, he turned his head. Catching sight of her, his blue eyes lit and his small lips curved upward. Her heart turned over. How such a blessing could come from her messed-up relationship with Wall never ceased to amaze her.

She stroked his cheek with the tip of her forefinger. "Hello, sweet boy."

Throwing off the quilt, she got out of bed. "Are you ready for a cuddle?"

His entire body wriggled with glee.

She picked him up and kissed his forehead. Carrying him over to the window, she held him in the crook of her arm. With her free hand, she pushed aside the curtain.

Last night's storm had transformed the landscape into a winter wonderland of snowcapped evergreens. The sun had just topped the ridge, casting a reflective glow on the fresh-fallen snow.

The ground outside remained undisturbed, except for a single pair of tracks leading to the barn. Farmers rose early, too. Luke was already up and about.

If he hadn't come along last night… She didn't like to think what might have happened to them exposed to the elements in the middle of nowhere.

Getting an idea of how she might begin to repay him for his kindness, she dressed quickly and attended to Jeremiah's needs.

She slipped into the kitchen and buckled her

baby into an infant bouncy seat. Yet another attic find by Luke's mother. The Morgans didn't believe in throwing anything away. She set Jeremiah on the floor where he could watch her and went to work putting breakfast together.

When the back door creaked open, a blast of wintry air swept inside. Stomping his boots on the mat, Luke toed out of them before crossing into the kitchen.

"Oh." His Adam's apple bobbed in his throat. "It's you."

She raised her eyebrows. "Good morning to you, too."

"I didn't mean…" He ran his hand over his head in a valiant attempt to finger comb his hair. "I didn't expect to see you so early this morning."

She stirred the eggs in the skillet. "I don't like to be idle. I hope you're ready for breakfast."

He frowned. Something he did a lot, she noticed. Maybe that was just what his face did whenever he looked at her. She tried not to take it personally.

"You didn't have to fix breakfast."

She cocked her head. "I wanted to. And I wanted to practice what I learned from Leo, the short-order cook at the café." She pointed the spatula at him. "No biggie."

He sniffed the air. "Is that coffee?" he asked, shrugging out of his coat.

She transferred the steaming scrambled eggs

and several sausages to a blue porcelain plate. "Pour yourself a cup. I hope you like it strong. Like Kara makes at the café."

"I love the coffee at the café."

Jeremiah broke into gurgles.

She smiled. "He knows your voice. He's trying to talk to you."

Luke gave the bouncy seat and her son a wide berth as he headed to the counter, mug in hand. "Uh…okay. Sure."

She carried the plate to Luke's spot at the end of the table.

He lifted the carafe from the coffeemaker. "Can I get you a cup?"

She flitted to the counter. "You don't have to wait on me. I'll get it myself." She and Luke grabbed for the same empty mug.

"You don't have to wait on me, either."

An emotion filled his eyes but disappeared too quickly for her to identify.

Was it just her, or had it suddenly become rather warm? "I like working." She resisted the urge to fan her cheeks. "It's nice to be the one who helps people."

"Instead of being the other way around?"

Her breath hitched. "Yes, I suppose that's right."

Luke's forehead furrowed. "I can understand that."

She had the insane impulse to touch her finger

to his face and smooth out the crease. Her pulse leaped. His gaze bored into hers.

Breathe. Don't forget to br—

As if suddenly becoming aware that only a coffee cup was between them, he let go of the mug and stepped away. Padding in his socks to the table, he pulled out the chair and sat down.

Giving her heart a chance to settle, she concentrated on filling her mug. She placed her coffee on the table beside Luke and then angled Jeremiah so he could see them. She took a seat.

He dug his fork into the food. "Thanks."

"You're welcome."

He looked at her, chewing slowly. "Aren't you going to eat something?"

She shrugged. "Later. I thought I'd chat with you before you head outside again. Unless of course, you'd prefer to be alone." Gripping the handle of the mug, she half rose.

He placed his hand over hers. "I don't mind the company." His tanned cheeks flushed, and he withdrew his hand, resting it in his lap.

Shayla's heart thudded. Eyes dropping to the plate, he stuffed a forkful of eggs in his mouth. She took a sip of coffee to occupy herself. "What are your plans for the day?"

"An early-bird client is stopping by to cut their Christmas tree." He speared a sausage. "Later this morning, I've got to take this year's fir tree to the

Truelove square for the tree lighting in a couple of weeks."

She leaned forward. "Can I help?"

He picked up his coffee. "I'm only the delivery service. The Parks Department sets it up in the gazebo." He peered at her over the rim of the mug. "But I've done something you're probably not going to like."

Shayla's heart skipped a beat. Had Wall tracked her down?

"Last night, I called my friend from the firehouse, Zach Stone."

She'd forgotten Luke was a part-time firefighter with the Truelove Fire Department.

"I asked him to tow your car to his shop this morning."

She stiffened. "I can't pay for a tow, and besides, the car's not worth repairing." Suppose Zach ran the VIN number and discovered the car didn't belong to her?

"It had to be done." Luke set his jaw. "The vehicle was a traffic hazard where it was."

She glowered at him.

"While I'm in town, I'll swing by Zach's shop and get the kid's car seat, too."

Not once had Luke said Jeremiah's name or made any attempt to interact with him. Most people found her son irresistible. Not Luke Morgan.

Did his disapproval of her mistakes extend to

her child, as well? Jeremiah was not a mistake. Or perhaps Luke just didn't like children. Not everyone did. Maybe he didn't have much experience with babies and felt awkward around them.

Could be he just didn't like her, though, and wanted to keep his distance from both of them. Her stomach knotted. It surprised and saddened her that he would be so judgmental. Her failures were certainly not Jeremiah's fault.

But it wasn't the first time she'd been the object of either pity or disgust. She should've stayed far, far away from Truelove.

Pushing back a sob, she rose. The noise startled Jeremiah. His face puckered, and he started to cry. Kneeling, she unbuckled him and lifted him out of the seat.

"Shh… Mama's here." Cradling him close to her heart, she buried her face in his tiny sprouts of hair. "Don't wake the house, baby boy. Shh."

The stairs squeaked. She and Luke glanced up. Emily Morgan smiled.

"How long have you been standing there, Mom?"

Shayla rocked her small son. "I'm so sorry we woke you, Mrs. Morgan."

Luke's mother fluttered her hand. "It was long past time for me to be out of bed." Her gaze swung from her son to Shayla. "But don't you all look a right treat."

Surely his mom wasn't implying…

Nobody in their right mind would want Shayla and her fatherless child as part of their family. Certainly not with her only son.

Grunting, Luke scraped back his chair, sending Jeremiah into another spasm of crying.

Making a face, Luke bolted for the door. "Got to check th-the…" He grabbed his coat and his boots. "Tractor… The barn… The—" With a firm click, he closed the door behind him.

Now she'd chased the man from his own home.

She repositioned her son against her shoulder. His tummy felt hard. Maybe he was having a spell of gas.

Emily headed toward the stove. "You fixed breakfast, too? My girls need to take a page out of your playbook. Whatever will I do without you when you're gone?"

The coil in her gut pulled tighter. She had a feeling Luke wouldn't share his mother's sentiment. The sooner Monday came, the better. For all of them.

Rubbing small circles on Jeremiah's back, she crooned one of the mountain lullabies her mother used to sing. Until, fed up with the grinding poverty, one day she simply walked out the door. Shayla never saw her mother again.

But from the moment she'd felt the first flutter of life in her womb, like the quivering of a sparrow's wings, she'd known she'd never do what her mama had done.

"What a lovely voice you have."

She looked up. "Thank you."

Emily tilted her head. "Have you done much singing?"

Shayla continued to make small strokes on Jeremiah's back. He'd become content, calmed by the soothing sound of her singing. "Not since I was in high school."

Daddy hadn't liked to hear her sing. It reminded him of her mother and why she'd left them. Wall hadn't liked her to open her mouth and talk, period, much less sing.

She'd never had much to sing about. For most of her life, she'd kept the song inside her, not wishing to give her daddy anything else to resent about her.

The blond hair, the blue eyes, the petite stature—she looked enough like her mother as it was. No need to rub salt into raw wounds. But from the moment the delivery nurse placed her baby in her arms, she couldn't contain the songs that burst forth spontaneously from her heart.

"It's a shame you won't be here long enough to participate in the Christmas service." Emily inserted several slices of bread into the toaster. "Our church music director would love to have a voice like yours in the choir."

Shayla would've enjoyed that, too. But it was

important to get across the state line. And if all went well? Her voice might be her ticket—and Jeremiah's—to a better life.

When Luke returned from town, he found his mother and Shayla hard at work in the farm store making wreaths. Neither the baby nor his sisters were around.

"Zach wondered if you'd be interested in him scrapping the car for spare parts," Luke said. "He'd split the profit with you."

Shayla rested her hands on the table. "Please tell him I am interested in doing that."

"Look at the wreaths Shayla has put together." His mother gestured at the lattice wall now filled with greenery. "She's a natural."

He frowned. "Where are Caroline and Krista? This is supposed to be their project."

"Caroline is expecting a phone call from her boyfriend so she returned to the house to wait for it."

His thoughts on Caroline's current college boyfriend were best left unexpressed.

"So she left you and Shayla with the work," he growled.

His mom pursed her lips. "The house gets better reception than out here."

Shayla finished tying the garland around the circular wire frame. "Caroline's also making more bows and putting together lunch."

"And what about Krista?"

"She wanted to play with Jeremiah so we traded places." Shayla rose from the workbench. "Should I not have done that? Krista would probably be better with the wreaths."

Now he felt like a bully. He crimped the brim of his ball cap. "Krista wouldn't have done a better job." He grimaced. "Despite having done this work every November for Open House since Dad died."

His mother rose. "You push them too hard and expect too much. This is supposed to be their Thanksgiving break."

"And when do you and I get a break, Mom?"

Shayla's gaze ping-ponged between them.

"You make the farm a drudgery to them." His mother planted her hands on her hips. "They're young and should be allowed to enjoy life."

"From the last few years of bills, it looks like they've been enjoying university life." He gritted his teeth. "And they're both older than I was when I had to take over the responsibility for everything from Dad." He flung his arms wide.

Shayla flinched.

His mom's eyes glittered. "I'm sorry we've been such a burden to you."

Luke scrubbed his face with his hand. "That's not what I meant."

His mother strode toward the door. "Wasn't it?"

She left an awkward silence in her wake.

"Why does no one understand how hard I'm working to keep a roof over their heads?"

"Is it really that bad?" Shayla whispered.

"Yeah, it really is." He pinched the bridge of his nose. "This isn't the first time Mom and I have had this conversation. But I'm ashamed you witnessed me losing my temper."

Shayla laid her hand on his sleeve. "This is what you call losing your temper?"

Even through the heavy fabric of the coat, he felt her fingers, and his pulse leaped.

"Where I come from, darlin', we call that polite table conversation." She dropped her hand from his arm. "I should go check on Jeremiah."

She was heading up the path before he realized what she'd called him. Then he was out the door and following her to the house. Not because he liked being with her, of course, but because it was lunchtime and he was hungry.

His mood was not improved when he discovered that alongside his mom's homemade brown bread, they were eating the vegetable beef soup Shayla had fixed after he left for town. So much for Caroline's contribution to lunch.

Later, he was near the barn when a bronze Chevy ventured down the long, graveled drive to the house. Sam Gibson pulled to a stop in the grass next to the barn.

Sam and his new wife, Lila, exited the vehicle

with Sam's five-year-old daughter, Emma Cate. He, Sam and Lila had been in the same year at school. "Hey, man."

"Hey, yourself."

Sam had asked if he could bring Lila's great-aunt IdaLee Moore out to the farm on Wednesday to cut a tree. Her family had a Thanksgiving tradition of decorating the tree together.

The former high school quarterback shook Luke's hand. "Thanks for letting us stop by before Open House."

"No problem."

Lila smiled. "My aunt and uncle usually pick it up on their way to Thanksgiving dinner, but since Sam has a truck and he's part of the family now..."

She and Sam exchanged a sweet look that stole Luke's breath. His friend had never looked happier or more content. For a second, Luke wished a similar happiness for himself. Then he remembered he didn't have time for a woman in his life.

But maybe one day...

His gaze drifted toward the house. Through the windows, he could see Shayla and his mom cleaning up after lunch. As usual, if there was work to be done, his sisters were nowhere to be found.

In high school, he, Sam and the artsy, flame-haired Lila hadn't been in the same group of friends. Yet despite being one of the most popular guys on campus, Sam had always been unfailingly nice to everyone, including quiet, bookish, not-good-with-girls Luke.

After graduation and a stint in the Navy, Sam had struggled to build his now-successful paint contracting business at the same time Luke found himself wrestling with the operation of the tree farm. Sam had been a sounding board and a good friend ever since.

Emma Cate yanked open the rear door, and Sam helped the diminutive, very proper old woman step out of the truck.

Luke hurried forward. "Miss IdaLee, welcome."

Married, divorced or spinster, "Miss" was an honorary title of respect bestowed on any Southern lady who was your elder.

"Thank you, young Morgan, for allowing us to get our tree early."

Over the course of nearly four decades, the retired schoolteacher had taught everyone in Truelove. Including Luke. He glanced over to the house.

Would Shayla come out to greet her old teacher? He wasn't sure what to make of Shayla. Had she always been so skittish and he'd just never noticed?

"Emma Cate has never had the opportunity to cut her own Christmas tree." Her snow-white hair in a bun, IdaLee's violet-blue eyes twinkled. "A situation that needed to be rectified. Posthaste."

Yep. Posthaste. Rectified. That's how Miss Ida-Lee talked. He had it on good authority—from her new great-nephew Sam—she even texted in the Queen's English.

"Sam told me what size Fraser you're looking for." Luke motioned toward the trees that marched up the hills on three sides of the barn in straight lines like toy soldiers. "I've got a few in mind if you want to head this way."

"Move over, IdaLee!"

To Luke's surprise, another elderly woman climbed out of the truck.

GeorgeAnne Allen, an angular, faintly terrifying lady with ice-blue eyes and a short, iron-gray cap of hair, cast a critical glare over the rows of trees. "In my opinion, Christmas trees have become wildly overpriced."

Looking sheepish, Sam pulled at his chin. "When the Double Name Club heard we were headed this way…"

Emma Cate tugged at Sam's hand. "Can we go see de Chwistmas twees now, Daddy?"

"Yoo-hoo!"

Sure enough, where there was one, Truelove citizens could expect to find all the Double Name Club members—also known as the Truelove Matchmakers. The older ladies were infamous for poking their powdered noses where they didn't belong. They took the town motto—Truelove, Where True Love Awaits—a little too seriously.

Lila gave the last member of the matchmaking

trio a hand out of the truck. Pleasantly plump with salt-and-pepper hair, ErmaJean Hicks was as apple round as GeorgeAnne was spare.

"Just smell the evergreen scent in the air." ErmaJean took a swift breath. "So invigorating. So bracing. So Christmas—" Inhaling too deeply, she dissolved into a coughing fit.

GeorgeAnne rolled her eyes. "For the love of Fraser firs, ErmaJean."

Eyes watering, ErmaJean put her hand to her throat. "I'm so p-parched." She sputtered. "The c-cold m-mountain air at this elevation…"

The back door to the farmhouse flew open. Shayla ran out with a bottle of water. "Miss Erma-Jean, drink this." Unscrewing the lid, she thrust the bottle into the older woman's hand.

IdaLee's wrinkled face eased into a smile. "Shayla, child." The old lady gave her a hug. "I heard you were back in town."

"How?" Shayla's eyes widened. "I mean, you did?"

Something, not unlike the look of a hunted animal, flitted across her features.

"I was quite concerned about you last June when you left the café so suddenly." IdaLee's shrewd old eyes must have seen the same thing in Shayla's face as Luke had. "Not to worry." She patted Shayla's arm. "Zach at the repair shop is also my great-nephew. Before we leave this afternoon, I'd love to meet your baby."

Luke scowled. Zach and his big mouth. Although, to be fair, he hadn't known not to broadcast Shayla's whereabouts. And as to why that needed to remain a secret, Luke had no clue. But it unsettled him.

Emma Cate caught hold of Lila's hand. "Pwease, Mommy. Chwistmas twee."

"I think the child's been patient long enough." ErmaJean opened her hand, and Shayla deposited the bottle cap into her palm. "Thank you, dear heart, for your kindness."

"For once, ErmaJean's right." GeorgeAnne shooed Sam toward the fir-lined ridge. "Take your family to find IdaLee's tree." She turned a steely gaze upon Luke. "I'm sure Mr. Morgan can help me find the perfect tree for my gentleman friend, the judge."

GeorgeAnne was the bossy one. Although, when dealing with the matchmakers, that was splitting hairs. Thankfully, he'd never been caught in their machinations.

"She means her not-so-secret boyfriend, Walter." ErmaJean winked at Luke. "Isn't that right, Georgie?" she smirked.

The no-nonsense leader of the matchmaker pack

blushed like a schoolgirl. "You're one to talk. What about *your* gentleman caller, ErmaJean Hicks?"

"Bill is a retired school administrator." Erma-Jean batted her lashes. "And such a lovely man."

Luke and Shayla exchanged amused glances. A tactical error. He should've known the matchmakers wouldn't miss it.

"What about you, young Morgan?" IdaLee demanded. "What's taking you so long to find the love of your life?"

GeorgeAnne pulled a face. "He probably doesn't even have a girlfriend."

ErmaJean gave him a benevolent smile. "But he does have a nice truck."

He shuffled his boots on the gravel. "How about I get the golf cart so you ladies can ride in style to inspect the trees?"

"That's very considerate." IdaLee gave her compatriots a significant look. "He'll make someone an extraordinary husband."

ErmaJean hugged Shayla's arm. "Did you hear that, dear heart?"

"So what are you waiting for already, Morgan?" GeorgeAnne glared. "Easter?"

Hurrying toward the shed to retrieve the cart, he congratulated himself on dodging a bullet. He felt only a small pang of conscience at leaving Shayla alone in their clutches, caught like a deer in headlights. But when it came to the matchmakers, it was every man or woman for themselves.

Quiet by nature, he was an observer. And what he'd observed thus far hadn't made him want to rush headlong into marriage. Truth was, he'd never felt the way Sam looked at his new bride.

Even if a tiny part of him envied that, the drama such feelings brought was enough to give a rational, calm person like himself the willies.

He drove the cart over to the Double Name Club ladies. Not unexpectedly, GeorgeAnne climbed into the front passenger seat. Shayla helped the other two women into the back seat.

ErmaJean leaned forward. "Just what kind of girl are you looking for, Luke, honey?"

"This is your chance to set the record straight." IdaLee rapped him on the shoulder. "We aim to please."

Shayla did a poor job at muffling a laugh. "Yes, do tell us, Luke, *honey.*"

Wait until they started on her. Then she'd see how hilarious it was being cornered by the Double Name Club.

"I'm looking for a simple, uncomplicated, sturdy woman to work the farm with me."

Shayla arched her eyebrow. "That's the dumbest thing I ever heard."

He scowled. "Oh, really?"

"Yes, really." She curled her lip. "You don't want a wife. You want a plow horse."

Ouch. Untrue.

The older women hooted.

"It's not dumb." It sounded dumb coming out of his mouth, but Luke wasn't one for quick repartee. He was no good with the flashy comebacks.

They left Shayla behind at the farmhouse. He got busy helping the ladies make their selections and cut their trees. Finally, a few hours later, he stood in the barnyard as Sam drove away. The truck was loaded down with several Christmas trees, assorted garlands and a menagerie of meddling matchmakers.

Crossing the yard, he met Shayla coming out of the house.

"Krista's watching Jeremiah. I'm going to finish the rest of the wreaths at the store with Caroline and your mom." She stopped on the path next to him. "I saved you a brownie."

She'd made brownies? His mouth watered. But there was no rest for weary Christmas tree farmers the week of Thanksgiving.

"I've got a few things to do to get ready for Friday. You know how it is with us plow horses." He gave her a slightly crooked smile. "We just trudge on."

She laughed. And his treacherous heart thumped.

Wiggling her fingers over her shoulder, she continued on her way.

He sighed. For both their sakes, he intended to stay far, far away from Shayla. Although, that might be easier said than done.

Chapter Four

On Thanksgiving morning, Luke's mom and his sisters managed to beat Shayla into the kitchen. Jeremiah in her arms, she paused on the bottom step of the staircase.

Flour on her hands, Caroline rolled out a piecrust on the kitchen island. "Mornin' to my favorite little guy in the world."

The baby gurgled at the sound of their voices.

Shayla came off the last step with her son. "Jeremiah says good morning to you, too."

Krista wiped her hands on a dish towel and reached for him. "Can I feed him his rice cereal?"

She handed him into Krista's eager arms. Jeremiah would miss the attention after they left Truelove. Her, too. Single parenting wasn't easy. She hadn't been so well rested since before he was born.

Emily looked up from a cookbook. "Happy Thanksgiving."

Shayla moved into the kitchen. "How can I help?"

"I'm sure we'll find something for you to do soon enough." Emily opened the refrigerator and removed a stick of butter. "But first help yourself to coffee and doughnuts."

Shayla kept an eye on Krista, but there was really no need. Luke's sister had heated a bottle of formula and then tested its temperature on her wrist, just as she'd watched Shayla do.

Caroline swiped the back of her hand across her cheek, leaving a streak of flour. "We eat light Thanksgiving morning. Gotta save room for the feast."

"Apple cider doughnuts from Callie McAbee at the Apple Valley Orchard—our Thanksgiving treat." Holding Jeremiah, Krista poured formula into the rice cereal and stirred. "It's amazing what you have to learn to do with one hand, isn't it?"

Shayla laughed. "You've already become a pro."

Krista settled Jeremiah into the high chair. Her son looked so big, sitting up by himself. Seeing the bowl, Jeremiah banged his chubby fists on the tray. At the loud noise, his eyes went wide.

The women froze, holding their breath, expecting tears. But he banged his hands again and laughed, apparently realizing he was making the noise. They all laughed, too.

"You are such a funny, cuddly bear." Krista sat next to him and held out the spoon. Like a little bird, his mouth popped open.

Emily set the microwave timer to melt the butter in a bowl. "Because Open House is the next day, Thanksgiving tends to be low-key for us, but we do have turkey and everybody gets to pick a favorite side dish."

Caroline managed to skillfully transfer the dough crust to the pie plate. "My vote is for Mom's special corn pudding."

"My choice is always deviled eggs." Krista held the spoon halfway to Jeremiah's mouth. "Deviled eggs are appropriate for every occasion. What do you think, Shayla?"

She took a sip of coffee. "I agree."

Leaning forward to meet the spoon, Jeremiah grunted.

"Sorry, snuggle bunny." Slipping the rice into his mouth, Krista winked at her. "My mistake in getting between a guy and his food."

Jeremiah slapped his hands on the tray again and grinned, a ring of white cereal around his lips.

Emily planted a quick kiss on his forehead. "Every year I ask for pumpkin pie."

Caroline crimped the edges of the crust. "And every year, I make it for her."

At the ding, Emily removed the melted butter from the microwave. "Luke always requests green bean casserole."

There was no sign of Luke. But somehow she'd known he wasn't in the kitchen before she was halfway down the stairs. When it came to him, it was like she had a supercharged antenna.

If he was nearby, she got this odd sensation. And when he wasn't, no goose bumps. No heightened awareness. No uptick in her pulse. Nothing.

Which was weird. And not something she'd ever admit aloud. She'd lain in bed for far too long last night thinking about the Christmas tree farmer.

She broke a chunk off a doughnut. He must be outside on the farm. Already hard at work. She chewed.

He was the hardest working man she'd ever met, although considering her lazy excuse for brothers and dad, that might not be saying much. Still, last spring at the café she'd also had occasion to observe the fire chief, who'd spent a lot of time courting her boss, Kara. Will MacKenzie was the kind of man she wished her father and brothers had been.

Luke was a great brother, that much was obvious. Not that she thought of him as a brother. Or felt even a bit sisterly toward him.

She wasn't sure what she felt for Luke, which was a matter of grave concern to her. It never worked getting too attached to people. Most especially, not someone like Luke.

"What side would you like for the Thanksgiving feast, Shayla?"

"I get a pick, too?"

"Of course." Emily smiled. "Everyone gets a say-so in the family meal. That's how it works."

Except Shayla wasn't family. "I don't know. What kinds of stuff do people serve at Thanksgiving dinner?"

Krista's forehead wrinkled. "You've never been to a Thanksgiving dinner?"

Caroline threw her sister a scathing glance.

Shayla flushed. "We…my family…there wasn't—"

"Choose anything you like." Caroline gave her a gentle smile. "As long as the ingredients are in the pantry, the sky's the limit. If you've got a hankering for pigs in a blanket, I see no harm in eating them for Thanksgiving."

Shayla was unable to imagine the willow-thin Caroline Morgan actually eating baby hot dogs. But she appreciated her kindness in overlooking her ignorance of Thanksgiving rituals.

"Before my grandmother died—I was really young and I'm not sure if it was Thanksgiving or not—but I think I remember a dish she made that had sweet potatoes."

"Excellent choice." Caroline smiled. "Sweet potato casserole. Classic Thanksgiving fare."

She chewed her lip. "Are you sure? I think there were marshmallows on top, too."

Emily pulled open the pantry. "Marshmallows are not a problem."

Shayla poked her head inside. An entire shelf bulged with bags of marshmallows.

"We sell hot chocolate during Open House weekend."

Krista wiped Jeremiah's mouth with a wet cloth. "Can I carry him around in that sack thing while we make lunch?"

Caroline rolled her eyes. "She means the baby sling."

Shayla hurried forward to slide back the tray and unbuckle Jeremiah from the high chair. "If that would make you happy…"

Krista's cheeks lifted. "Being with baby Jeremiah makes me deliriously happy." She clasped her hands under her chin. "The happiest girl in Truelove. The most—"

"Drama queen much, little sis?" Caroline smirked.

Shayla propped her son against her shoulder, rubbing small circles on his back. "I left the sling in the bedroom on the—"

Krista pounded up the stairs.

"—dresser." Shayla bit back a smile. "She's a great babysitter."

Caroline poured the pureed pumpkin mixture into the pie shell. "She'd make an even better aunt."

Shayla nearly choked on her coffee. Were Caroline and her boyfriend that serious? Or was Caroline referring to Luke? Did he have someone special—a simple, uncomplicated, sturdy woman to work the farm with him—in his life?

Well, of course he must. The girls around here weren't idiots. Or, based on their nosy questions yesterday, perhaps the matchmakers had someone particular in mind for him. But simple and uncomplicated, Shayla was not.

She set her mug on the table. It wasn't any of her business whether Luke was involved with someone. Or who the matchmakers planned to set him up with. But it bothered her that it bothered her.

"I'm going to teach you how to make Luke's green bean casserole." Emily retrieved a can of green beans from the pantry. "Many hands make light work."

The rest of the morning flew by. The Thanksgiving feast was like nothing she'd ever experienced. Luke said a short blessing and then everyone dug into the food. Watching Luke and his family interact, she was struck that this was how it was supposed to be and what family was supposed to mean. The laughter. The bantering. The gentle teasing couched in love.

This was what she wanted for Jeremiah. Her

eyes brimmed with tears. This was what she wanted for herself.

Fastened in his high chair, Jeremiah's head bobbed. He jerked. His eyes widened and then narrowed again. His little fists opened and closed around a handful of mashed potatoes.

"Uh, Shayla." Luke pointed. "I think—"

Jeremiah fell face forward into the puddle of potatoes. Krista giggled. Shayla jumped up.

"Out like a light." Caroline grinned. "Not unlike Luke in the recliner."

Emily eased the tray away while Shayla carefully scooped up her sleeping child.

"It's called hard work." Luke cocked his head. "You should try it."

Caroline threw her napkin at him. He chuckled.

Emily cleaned Jeremiah's forehead and hands while Shayla held him in her arms. Luke volunteered himself and Krista to load the dishwasher and clear the table.

Shayla went upstairs to lay Jeremiah in the crib to finish out his nap. She turned on the baby monitor, another Morgan attic find. She took the receiver unit with her.

When she returned downstairs, she found the kitchen returned to its usual spic-and-span order.

Luke started the dishwasher. "Mom and Krista took the hot chocolate mix and marshmallows out to the farm store to set up for tomorrow morning."

She clipped the monitor to the loop on her jeans. "I can help them." She moved toward the mounted pegs where the family stashed their coats. "Jeremiah should be asleep for a couple of hours."

He stuffed his hands in his pockets. "I thought, if you wanted to, you could ride to town with me to check on the tree lot."

"I—I'd love to." Her eyes flitted toward the ceiling. "But I probably shouldn't leave—"

"I'll listen out for Jeremiah," Caroline called from the living room.

"A break would do you good." Luke shrugged into his overcoat. "And I'd enjoy your company."

She smiled. "Okay." She unclipped the monitor and left it with Caroline.

Pulling away from the house in Luke's truck, she felt nervous about leaving Jeremiah. They passed the little white outbuilding with the green shutters the Morgans called "the store."

Making wreaths there yesterday was the farthest she'd ever been away from her son. She gripped the armrest as the truck bounced along the graveled drive.

The truck lurched as he steered onto the road. "What's wrong?"

She braced against the door. "What if he wakes up and needs me?"

"Little guy's tuckered out." Luke threw her

a glance. "After eating his way through the mashed potatoes."

Her mouth twitched. "Single-handedly."

Luke threw her a grin. "Looked more like double-fisted to me."

Her breath caught in her throat. *Wow.* Maybe it was better he didn't smile at her too often.

Because when he did, the effect was transformative. He went from good-looking boy next door to downright handsome. And with the butterflies doing handstands in her belly, it unsettled her.

The truck ate up the miles between the farm and Truelove. They rode in silence, but it was a comfortable silence.

Entering the town limits, he motioned at the welcome sign. "Brand-new sign went up since you were here in the spring." The old one had been ripped away by the tornado.

"Says the same thing, though."

"Truelove—Where True Love Awaits." He made a face. "No thanks."

"You don't believe in true love?"

He shrugged. "By the time I get the farm in the black, marry off my sisters…"

She laughed.

"Don't laugh." He shook his head. "Those pesky sisters of mine require a great deal of supervision."

She loved the relationship he had with his sisters. It was not perfect, but sweetly endearing.

"By that time, I'll be ready for a rocking chair, not matrimony."

"I wouldn't be too sure." She batted her lashes. "I think the matchmakers have you in their sights. You're probably their next project."

He groaned. "Say it isn't so." The truck clattered over the bridge crossing the river. "What about you?"

"What about me?"

"Rocking chairs aren't only for the elderly." He smiled. "They rock babies, too. And there's nothing the matchmakers love more than putting together forever families."

She dropped her gaze. "Even if I weren't a Coggins, I'm damaged goods in most people's eyes."

Reaching across the seat, he grabbed hold of her hand. "Not in mine."

Her pulse quickened at his touch and his words.

"Don't sell yourself short. You're a great mom. You're smart and a hard worker."

The conversation had turned so personal. It was time to lighten the mood. "Are you about to compare me to a horse, Luke Morgan?"

He laughed as she'd intended. "No, but now that you mention it…"

She socked him in the arm.

He rubbed his biceps. "But seriously, any man would be blessed to have you and your son in his life. You have a lot to offer."

She regretted punching him. Mainly, though, because his hand was no longer on hers. *You are so losing it, girl.*

His gaze swung back to the road. "And you're beautiful." Beneath the beard stubble, a faint hint of red tinged his cheeks.

Luke Morgan thought she was beautiful? Her heart fluttered in her chest.

He drove past the vet clinic. "I'll give you the five-cent tour of the new and improved Truelove. Won't take long in this tiny Podunk town."

She elbowed him. "It's wonderful here."

"It's home." He winked. "And a virtual metropolis since we got that second streetlight."

She got her first look at the refurbished downtown that had been ravaged by the spring tornado. "Truelove looks great."

Luke gestured at the red-and-white-striped awning over the café on Main Street. "Were you part of the volunteer crew that helped put the Mason Jar together again for Kara?"

"I was." Shayla nodded. "How is Kara?"

"Since the newlyweds returned from their honeymoon in Paris, the guys at the fire station feel it's our civic duty to drop by the Jar each week to ensure the MacKenzies are living happily ever after." He gave her a lopsided smile. "And to make sure the chocolate croissants are living their best life in our bellies, too."

She rolled her eyes. "Thank you for the update, Mr. Romance."

He pointed out other changes as they drove the length of the square. "Big news. Kara and her mother, Glorieta, are expanding their operation. They bought the storefront over there."

Owner of a string of restaurants across the state, Glorieta Ferguson was known as the barbecue queen of North Carolina.

"Mama G's Down Home Barbecue and Fixins is opening a venue in Truelove?"

His mouth quirked. "Better than that."

"What could be better than Mama G's?"

"The Truelove grapevine says we're getting our own bakery soon. Pies. Cakes. Doughnuts." He smacked his lips. "The fire station can hardly wait." He rounded the corner of the square.

She rubbernecked at the village green. "You planted more trees."

"To supplement the ones we lost the day of the storm."

Eight-foot saplings dotted the gaps among the enormous oaks surrounding the square.

She caught a glimpse of white. "You rebuilt the gazebo, too?"

"Just a temporary structure till the town has enough money to hire a preservationist craftsman to re-create the historic details." He drove past Allen's Hardware. "You can't keep the good people of Truelove down for long."

"Truth you should take to heart." She looked at him. "I can tell you like living here."

"Never had the chance to know anywhere else." He frowned as they passed the darkened exterior of the bank. "Although if I don't get the loan extension for the farm…" His shoulders slumped. "Relocation will be my only option."

"Where would you go?"

"I don't have much in the way of marketable skills." He looked away. "Not a lot of demand for Christmas tree farmers without any land."

"You could go back to your writing." She hated to see him so down. "Everyone loved the stories you wrote for the school newspaper. You have a talent for finding the beauty in the ordinary. The stuff we take for granted."

"That doesn't pay the bills or put food on the table." His brow scrunched. "Let's talk about something else, if you don't mind."

She motioned toward the 3D Christmas lights lining the sidewalks. "It's beginning to look a lot like Christmas."

Mounted to the streetlights, large white plastic snowflakes sparkled in the afternoon sunshine. Red-ribboned wreaths bedecked Main Street businesses and the town hall.

"Just in time for Saturday's Christmas Parade and Santa on the Square." He pulled alongside the curb next to the tree lot across from the police station. "The Morgan Farm tree lot has a front row seat to the weekend festivities."

The usually empty parcel of land had been transformed into a winter wonderland miniature forest. Strings of twinkle lights lined the perimeter of the tree lot. They got out of the truck.

He guided her toward the winding footpath among the snow-covered clusters of Christmas trees. "Starting tomorrow, the farm will be open for choose-and-cut on the weekends, but for local customers who don't want the hassle, we offer pre-cut trees in town."

"I had no idea the prep work that went into Christmas trees." She followed him through the delightful maze of evergreens. "How long have you been getting ready for this weekend?"

"Used to be my dad and me. Now I hire a part-timer every September. A retired, older guy. We've been working nonstop to get the trees cut and shipped to a few wholesale customers who have their own lots farther away."

She lifted her face to inhale the tangy pine tree aroma filling the air.

He steered her toward a clearing in the center of the lot. "If only I'd been able to secure a contract with one of the national distributors, we wouldn't be facing foreclosure now."

"God will provide."

They emerged from the trees, and he stopped in front of a shiny aluminum camper on wheels. "Will He?"

She tilted her head. "Of course He will."

Luke flushed. "I guess I'm surprised to hear you say that."

"God sent you to rescue us during a snowstorm when I needed help the most, didn't He?" She touched his sleeve. "I have to believe He has something bigger in store for you. Better than you could imagine."

A smile teased at the corner of his lips. "I sure hope so, although I've got to warn you. A writer like me has a pretty good imagination." He blinked. "I can't believe I just called myself a writer."

"You are a writer. I wish you could see yourself the way others see you."

"Ditto for you, Shayla Coggins." He hitched his eyebrows. "A truth you should take to heart."

"Here you are, using my own words against me." She sighed. "You almost make me believe in the possibilities."

"And you remind me to never give up hope."

Luke was so easy to talk to. And fun. She

hadn't had much fun in her life. But when she was with him…

She brought her thoughts up short. Monday morning she'd be on a bus to Nashville. Their paths would likely never cross again.

All the more reason to savor the time she had with him now.

She gestured at the barrel, filled with kindling, in the center of the clearing. "I guess you light that at night."

"We do. It gets cold. And the camper serves as a warm refuge between customers." Removing a key from his pocket, he unlocked the camper door. "During the week, the part-timer and I take turns manning the tree lot. On the weekends when the farm is open for choose-and-cut, he works here without me."

"I wish I could see the town lit up at night."

On the camper steps, he turned back to her. "No reason you can't. We'll ride over here Saturday after dark. You and the kid can take in the Christmas lights."

"It's a date." She went crimson. "I mean… Your whole family would probably enjoy…" *Stop talking. Just stop talking.*

His mouth lifted in a half grin. "I'm sure Mom, Krista and Caroline will have lots of other things they'd rather do than take in the Truelove Christmas lights." He ducked his head to enter the camper. "But if they don't, I'm sure I can find something that needs doing in our absence."

Luke gave her another bashful grin. Goose bumps broke out on her arms. He disappeared inside the camper.

Had Luke asked her on a date? He probably didn't mean to imply it was a *date-date*. More likely he meant an appointment to put on the calendar. But either way...

Don't think too far into the future. Just enjoy the now with him.

He emerged from the camper holding a thick black marker and a bunch of blank white tags with strings.

"What can I do to help?"

"You have no idea how much you've already helped me by listening to me vent about the stuff I don't share with my family." He came down the steps. "Letting me think out loud gives me a better perspective."

She took the marker. "We're such a good influence on each other, we ought to be friends."

He gave her a slow smile. "We should."

The butterflies in her belly went into loop de loops. *That smile of his is a lethal weapon.*

"Okay, friend." He handed her a blank tag. "Help me price the Christmas trees."

As they walked around the lot, she hummed

the opening bars to "O Christmas Tree" under her breath. Just because she felt so happy.

But, already, a small, treacherous part of her heart wondered if friendship with Luke could ever possibly prove to be enough.

Chapter Five

On Friday, Open House started off with a parking lot full of cars. Good news for Luke's struggling bottom line. The families were eager to get the holidays off to a great start with a Morgan Farm Christmas tree.

He waved at AnnaBeth, her cowboy husband, Jonas, and their pint-size lasso champion son, Hunter. AnnaBeth had brought her mom, Victoria, and her dad along, too. Luke hurried over to offer his help.

Victoria was a Morgan Farm VIP. Last year, the Charlotte socialite and style maven had bought a half-dozen of his biggest trees for her large mansion. Later bedecked with elaborate decorations, the trees were featured in the *Christmas in Carolina* edition of a well-regarded Southern lifestyle magazine. AnnaBeth's mom had been kind enough to insist the journalist include the details of his operation in a sidebar.

The response had been positive. His de facto marketing specialist, Caroline, had fielded tons of emails. He had to believe the publicity would drive up sales over the next couple of weeks, which was crucial for the short Christmas tree season. He hoped the bank would take notice. He also hoped it wasn't too late for it to matter.

Business remained brisk all morning. His mom took charge of the storefront. Krista and Shayla handed out handsaws to customers and carts to haul the cut trees back to the parking lot. While he put the trees through the baler, his mother rang up their tickets inside the store.

Out on the broad-planked porch, Caroline served hot chocolate and marshmallows. He'd given his oldest sister the fun job today as a reward for the good deed she'd done Shayla on Thanksgiving.

Yesterday, when he and Shayla were in town, Callie McAbee and Miss ErmaJean had dropped by the tree lot with the gift of a front-facing baby carrier. Unbeknownst to either him or Shayla, Caroline had called around to find one for Jeremiah. Sturdy little Micah McAbee had outgrown the need for it.

"Enjoy your baby while you can." ErmaJean had winked at Shayla. "They're little such a short time."

He'd been impressed by his sister's thoughtfulness. Maybe she was maturing. Thinking of others, and not only herself. Perhaps one day, Caroline might prove to be a responsible adult, after all. That was his hope anyway.

As for never-met-a-stranger ErmaJean?

He hadn't liked the speculative gleam in the matchmaker's denim-blue eyes. Was Shayla right about him becoming the Double Name Club's next project?

Although, once any prospective girlfriends got a look at his mountain of debt and the hard work involved in living on a farm, they'd probably hightail it out of Truelove faster than Kris Kringle could say, "Ho ho ho."

Luke's gaze drifted over the farm until he located Shayla. His heartbeat quickened. She fit into the operation almost as if she'd been born to it.

His father had loved the farm. It was times like Open House that Luke missed his dad the most.

There were lots of people he didn't recognize this year. Flatlanders, he guessed, coming to the Blue Ridge for a Christmas tree.

He prayed they'd make it an annual holiday tradition at Morgan Farm. He also prayed Morgan Farm would still be around next year.

During a lull between customers, he cast an appreciative eye toward Shayla, who was going above and beyond to help their customers.

Not surprisingly, Krista had insisted on field-testing the baby carrier. He scanned the area until he spotted the telltale orange knit cap bobbing below Krista's throat as she wove her way among the rows.

Someday, his youngest, curly-haired sister would make a great mom. Like a Christmas Pied Piper, Krista was surrounded by a group of children as she played some sort of game with them among the trees.

The kid was cute. Adorable even. Which made it even more necessary for Luke to guard his heart. The little guy tugged on his heartstrings in a way he'd never imagined possible. With the baby out of his life in three more days, all the more reason for Luke to keep his distance.

Carrying a tray, Caroline came out on the porch to pass around steaming cups of cocoa to apple orchard farmer Jake McAbee, his wife Callie, and their two children.

His baby sisters were growing up. And the idea of launching them into an unsuspecting society didn't give him as much pleasure as it once did. He absolutely needed to start thinking about getting a life of his—

"Luke!" Krista screamed. "I need help! Luke!"

His head snapped up.

"Somebody help me get him out of this thing!" Racing toward him, she struggled with the carrier buckles under her arms. "Jeremiah's choking!"

Throwing down the tree he was threading through the machine, he took off running toward her. Jake sprinted after him, hard on his heels, but Luke reached Krista first.

Gasping for air and making a high-pitched sound, Jeremiah had turned blue.

"One of the children gave him a peppermint before I could stop her. And everything that goes in his hand goes into his mouth." Tears poured down Krista's face as she fumbled with the Velcro. "He can't breathe. I can't—"

Luke ripped the straps off her body. The child went limp in his arms. Luke went down on one knee.

Shayla rushed forward, but Miss IdaLee caught hold of her. "Luke is a trained EMT. Let him work, child."

Using his thigh for support, he placed the baby facedown on his forearm. With the heel of his free hand, he delivered five quick, strong blows to the area between Jeremiah's shoulder blades. Each time he struck the boy, Shayla flinched.

On the fifth stroke, the hard candy popped out of Jeremiah's mouth. The child gave a lusty, full-throated wail. Cheers arose from the gathered crowd.

He turned the baby over. Her face pale, Shayla reached for him. He laid the child into the comfort of her waiting arms.

"Thank you, Luke." She held her baby close. "You saved his life."

"It happened so quickly." Trembling from head to toe, Krista's eyes flooded with tears. "I couldn't see his face. I couldn't get it out of his mouth. I—I—"

Luke pulled Krista into a hug.

Her big brown eyes reminded him of the woebegone little girl she'd once been when a beloved dog had run away. And the heartbroken middleschooler who'd stood beside him at their father's fresh grave.

"You did the exact right thing, Krissy." His sister was in need of at least as much comfort as Jeremiah. "You got him to me. He's going to be fine. See?"

They turned as Jeremiah's frightened wails turned from fear into a cry both of them recognized—hunger.

"I'm so sorry, Shayla," Krista rasped.

He watched the emotions play over Shayla's expressive features and saw the moment the spunk, which had enabled her to survive a lifetime of trouble, gained the upper hand.

"Things happen." Shayla's face cleared. "We deal. We pray. And we get back on the horse that threw us."

His throat clogged. This was why he was so attracted to Shayla Cogg—*whoa*. Where had that come from?

She threw him a smile. "You caught the horse reference?"

"I—I did." He rubbed his neck. "What doesn't kill us, makes us stronger?"

"Something like that." She plopped her baby into Krista's arms. "He cries on your watch—you get to feed him lunch and make him happy again."

He hoped his gratitude showed for how she handled the situation. Shayla's reaction could have scared Krista off kids for life. Instead of anger and recriminations, she'd given his sister the grace and mercy Krista needed most.

Shayla Coggins was a remarkable person.

Elbowing him, Krista rocked the baby. "Can't we pretty please just keep her, big bro?" she whispered. "A new sister is all I want for Christmas." She headed for the farmhouse with Jeremiah.

All he wanted for Christmas, too. Wait. What was with him?

Raking his hand over his face, he hoped Shayla hadn't overhead his sister. But from the narrowing of her violet-blue eyes, he had a sneaking suspicion Miss IdaLee had.

The crowd dispersed. His mom and the McAbees went inside the store. On the porch, Caroline remained in deep conversation with AnnaBeth's mother, Victoria. He didn't have time to wonder what that was about, however, because another family waited for him at the baler to finish wrapping their tree.

As soon as he helped the guy load the tree into his vehicle, he searched for Shayla. She'd returned to handing out carts and handsaws. Stepping away from the machine, he touched her shoulder. "Shay—"

Shrieking, she jerked.

He froze, his hand still midair. "I thought you saw me walking over. I—"

"I didn't realize it was you." She crossed her arms.

He felt terrible for startling her. "I didn't mean to scare you."

"I'm fine. No harm."

She didn't look fine. Her blue eyes were wide, her palpable fear far out of proportion unless... A sinking feeling squeezed his gut.

"Did someone hurt you, Shayla?"

Looking stricken, she turned away. He hated not being able to see her beautiful face.

She made a vague, fluttery motion with her hand. "It's not a big deal. I'm fine, really."

He felt stupid for not realizing before.

"Shayla, I hope you know I'd never hurt you."

He made a move to touch her arm and stopped himself just in time. Flushing, he dropped his hand. "I didn't stop to think. I'm such an idiot. Coming up on a woman like that. I—"

She grabbed his hand. "I know you wouldn't hurt me. I may not know a lot, but I know that much, Luke Morgan."

He swallowed. "Then I apologize on behalf of the rest of my gender."

She squeezed his hand so hard he winced. "You of all people have absolutely nothing to be sorry for with me. Nothing at all."

He wasn't sure what she meant by that.

"Thank you for caring, Luke."

Rising on the toes of her boots, she brushed her lips across his cheek. His heart went into overdrive. The sweet scent of vanilla wafted from her. Letting go of his hand, she came down on the heels of her boots.

She gave him a fleeting smile. "I should go check on my boy, but I'll be back as quick as I can."

His senses overwhelmed by her, his head swam. He watched her pick her way past the store to the farmhouse.

"Such a fierce little thing, isn't she?" Bright as a winter cardinal in her ruby red coat and hat, Miss IdaLee leaned against the fence post draped with garland. "But then, our Shayla has had to be, hasn't she?"

His gaze flicked toward the farmhouse. "Didn't

expect to see you again since you've already bought your Christmas tree, Miss IdaLee."

"I needed more garland for the railing on my veranda." The retired schoolteacher touched a hand to her snow-white hair. "My niece Myra Penry and her husband, Cliff, gave me a ride to the farm."

Luke had stopped trying to count IdaLee's nieces and nephews, much less keep track of the legion of grandnieces and grandnephews, which included Jonas, Zach and Lila. The elderly maiden lady was related to half the county.

"In high school, why didn't I recognize the signs?" He clenched his fists. "She's a victim of physical abuse."

"Because you were just a kid yourself." IdaLee frowned. "And don't call her a victim. She's not. She's a survivor."

"I'm guessing it was at the hands of her father."

"Which took the form of poverty and neglect."

Barely recalled images of the younger Shayla floated through his mind. Pieces to a puzzle that only now began to make sense.

He gritted his teeth. "Why didn't someone get her out of there? Why didn't you help her?" He glared at the old woman.

"Before her mother abandoned them, she was the happiest child I ever saw." IdaLee knotted her gnarled blue-veined hands. "I communicated my concerns to the school administrator. Beverly

Jackson tried to intervene with the courts to remove the child from the home, but to no avail."

Callie McAbee's now-deceased mother had been a county social worker.

He gulped. "So what happened?"

"One of the greatest regrets of my life is that we weren't able to save her brothers. They were preteens when their mother left them. At a vulnerable age, they'd already started on the path which would eventually land them in prison."

Anger simmered in his belly. "Are you telling me Shayla fell through the cracks?"

"Her father, Adolphus Coggins, is a hard man. He fought us at every turn. Nothing could be proven. And Coggins had a way of scaring everyone off. But Maggie Hollingsworth's father, Tom, didn't give up."

Tom Arledge was Truelove's former police chief. Several years ago when he retired, his future son-in-law, Bridger Hollingsworth, was hired for the position.

"As police chief, Tom let Coggins know he was going to keep a watchful eye on Shayla, and that Dol's extralegal activities might not bear up well under scrutiny. Coggins is nothing if not a practical man. He was an indifferent father, but he lived up to his agreement with Tom. From then on, she always had food and a roof over her head."

"I'm not sure I'm buying that the abuse stopped

a long time ago." He jabbed his hands in his pockets. "You saw how frightened she became when I touched her." His mouth pinched.

The old woman looked at him. "From her instinctive reaction, the abuse is perhaps more recent."

He clamped his jaw tight. It made him physically ill to think of Shayla enduring such treatment.

"Why didn't she ever say anything?" He sagged against the fence post. "If Caroline or Krista found themselves in the same position, I pray someone would try to help them."

"Perhaps this is why the good Lord has seen fit to put her in your life." The octogenarian touched his sleeve. "I hope you don't think less of her because of this revelation."

"Of course not." He straightened. "If anything, I admire her all the more for the hurdles she's overcome."

IdaLee's voice quavered. "She's only ever had herself to depend upon. She's not comfortable trusting people. She's gotten used to everyone in her life letting her down when she needed them the most."

He closed his eyes.

IdaLee patted his arm. "Be patient and woo her gently."

His eyes flew open. Woo?

"And just maybe, the good Lord has put Shayla into your life for a reason, too." She wagged her bony finger at him. "As Scripture reminds us, 'Neglect not the gift that is in thee,' young Morgan."

He puffed out his chest. "I'm not sure what gift you think I'm neglecting. With all due respect, Miss IdaLee, I'm a Christmas tree farmer and Shayla's just a friend."

The schoolteacher laughed. "You keep telling yourself that, dear heart." The Penrys came out of the store with a small tabletop tree and an armful of garland. "Looks like my work here is done."

He surveyed the cars pulling into the lot on the hunt for Christmas trees. Hers might be. But his was certainly not.

That afternoon, conversation was awkward between him and Shayla. He missed their easy camaraderie. And as IdaLee had warned him, she appeared embarrassed by the earlier misunderstanding.

But he maintained a lighthearted banter and eventually coaxed her into a smile. His heart hammered. Wooing her… Was that what he was doing?

Later when he lost his hold on a tree trunk and the branches slapped him in the face, she laughed.

He spit out a mouthful of needles. "'O Christmas tree, O Christmas tree.'" He grimaced. "'How lovely are your branches.'"

And he was rewarded when she laughed at him again.

She held it upright so he could regain his grip on it. "I shouldn't have laughed. Are you all right?"

He grinned. "Worth it to see you smiling again." He hefted the tree into position on the machine. "Are we good? You and me?"

She tilted her head. "We're good."

The sun was setting by the time he loaded the last car with their Morgan Farm Christmas tree. Inside the store, his mom tallied the day's receipts. Shayla was restocking the shelves.

As he headed to the house, he shook his head. Always working, the woman was tough. Farm tough.

In the kitchen, he toed out of his boots. He could hear the shower running upstairs. Probably Krista. He ran a hand over his five-o'clock shadow. He could do with a shower and a shave.

His stomach growled. He'd grabbed a turkey sandwich around noon, but he'd long since burned through that. No sign of Caroline, who was supposed to be putting together Thanksgiving leftovers for supper.

Luke snagged a small piece of ham off a plate sitting on the counter. At a whirring sound, he turned. Sounded like the printer in his office.

He padded across the living room toward the light spilling from underneath the door to his office. Pushing the door wide, he poked his head inside and frowned. "Caroline? What're you doing?"

With a small cry, she jolted. Perched on her hip, Jeremiah's face puckered and he teared up.

Caroline scowled. "Now look what you've done. What were you thinking? Creeping up on us like that?"

"I wasn't creeping..." He planted his hands on his hips. "What's going on?"

She averted her gaze. "I had to finish something."

"Homework over Thanksgiving?"

What was going on with Caroline? He could always tell when she wasn't being entirely forthcoming with him. Had she failed to turn in a project on time? Was she in trouble with one of her professors?

Luke came around the desk, but before he could get a look at the monitor, she punched something on the keyboard and the screen went blank. Whirring to life again, the printer spit out more pages.

Her gaze flitted to the machine and back to him. Rubbing his eyes, Jeremiah made the monotonous whine that signified he was nearing the point of no return.

With the tray filling, Luke moved to scoop the papers before they fell to the floor. Somehow Caroline got between him and the printer, and she thrust the baby at him.

Out of reflex, he reached for the child.

"You heard Shayla's rules." With an interesting glint in her eye, Caroline grabbed the pages out of the tray. "You make him cry, you make him happy." She edged around him and made a bee-line for the door.

"Wait." His arms stiff and straight, he held the squalling baby away from him. "Where are you going?"

"For the love of Christmas trees, Luke." She shook her head. "He's not going to bite you."

"But what am I supposed to do with him?"

Rolling her eyes, she flipped her hair over her shoulder. "If you want dinner anytime soon, figure it out."

Then, to his horror, she was gone. And he was alone with the screaming infant.

"Uh…kid?" Holding the child the way he'd seen Caroline do, he bounced the baby on his hip. To no avail. "Hey, kid."

His face screwed tight with tiny tot rage, Shayla's son yelled his lungs out.

"Okay. I get it." He racked his brain for another solution. Where was his mother when he needed her? Or, for that matter, Jeremiah's mother? Getting desperate…

"Jeremiah…" He repositioned the child, rocking him in his arms. "Remember me? We're old buddies. Old pals from the event that hitherto—"

A writer word. Or else he was starting to sound like Miss IdaLee. But recognizing his name, the baby stopped crying.

"The event that, hitherto, shall be titled The Peppermint Candy Incident."

He blinked at Luke.

It was working. *Hallelujah and pass the corn bread*. It was working.

"That's right. You remember me, Jeremiah. Don't cry, little guy."

But then the infant scrunched his face again—

"Hey, hey. Don't start that again, Jeremiah."

The baby looked up at him. Like dewdrops, tears quivered on the tips of his lashes. His bottom lip trembled.

"I'm hungry and tired, too. Hangry is a dangerous combination. But I got to tell you a secret, little man." Luke held him closer as if to whisper in his ear. "The women on this farm have got us outnumbered. You and me, we've got to stick together."

He eased into his desk chair. "Since it's your first Christmas…"

The infant peered at him as if he understood every word.

"I know this isn't going to be the musical quality you're used to with your mom. 'Cause she's got a fabulous voice." He propped the baby on his shoulder and leaned back. "But while we're waiting for somebody to call us to dinner, we might as well get into the spirit of the season."

He hummed a few bars of a Christmas carol to find the pitch.

Jeremiah relaxed in his arms. Congratulating himself on latching on to something Jeremiah was familiar with, he softly launched into "Silent Night."

The "all is calm" part was not merely a line in the song, but his heartfelt prayer that the crying jag was behind them. Jeremiah made sweet, cooing noises.

His arms settled around the infant, Luke smiled. Such a cute baby. Luke closed his eyes and seamlessly segued—if he did say so himself—into "Away in a Manger."

The next time he opened his eyes, Shayla stood next to the chair. "Look at you two guys," she whispered. "All tuckered out."

His gaze shifted to the baby, lying against his shoulder. "Did Jeremiah fall asleep?"

The little boy stirred.

She picked up her son. "Not only him."

"I can't believe I fell asleep." He was surprised at how empty his arms felt when the baby went to Shayla. "I must've been more tired than I realized."

"No surprise to me." Eyes fluttering, the baby

arched and stretched in her arms. "You work harder than anyone I know."

Sitting upright, Luke rolled his head to work out the kinks in his neck. "No one works harder than you."

Eyes wide open, Jeremiah gave his mother the sweetest smile. Luke believed his heart might melt at the sight of them.

"Did you have a nice nap?" She placed her hand on Jeremiah's cheek. "Are you ready for dinner?"

"We did have a nice nap, thank you." Luke threw her a teasing grin. "And yes, we're definitely ready for dinner."

Burbling, the baby reached for him.

"Jeremiah knows your voice."

Getting out of the chair, he offered the baby his index finger. "You think so?" Jeremiah's tiny fingers curled around his. "Wow, what a grip."

She smiled. "It won't be easy to get him to let go."

Luke's mouth went dry. Despite the barriers and efforts to resist, the inevitable had happened. Somehow Jeremiah had also gotten a grip on his heart.

But, suddenly, he didn't mind so much. He wouldn't worry about Monday. Today's joy was sufficient. Such moments were rare and, therefore, all the more to be cherished.

A tiny pocket of perfect.

Chapter Six

If she lived to be a hundred, Shayla would never forget the sight of her child curled up against Luke in the office, both of them sound asleep. It made her weepy just thinking about it.

Was there anything sweeter than a strong man cradling a baby in his arms?

Unfortunately for Luke, Saturday did not get off to a good start. He received an early-morning text from the part-timer he'd hired to manage the tree lot in town. The retiree had thrown out his back yesterday. He was done for the season.

This sent Luke into a grim panic. "Fifty percent of our tree lot season happens during the festival today." He rubbed his forehead as if he had a headache. "I'll have to spend the day in town and cancel choose-and-cut at the farm."

"Nonsense. The girls and I can handle choose-

and-cut here." Emily's glance included Shayla, warming her. "Right, ladies?"

"But the baler," he protested.

Shayla set her coffee mug on the table. "If you show me, I'm sure I can run the baler."

Luke shook his head. "The bigger trees are too heavy for you to lift into the machine."

Krista curled her biceps. "Don't underestimate us, big bro."

"We'll help Shayla. Together we can do anything." Caroline fed Jeremiah a spoonful of mashed banana. "That's what family does. We help each other."

Leaning against the kitchen counter in her bathrobe, Emily smiled. "Exactly."

The baby grabbed for the spoon. Caroline let him play with it.

Family. Shayla ducked her head over her plate. It wasn't true. But to even be considered in the same category as family was beyond anything she could ever have hoped for.

"I won't let you down, Luke. I promise," she whispered.

A funny, endearing half smile lifted his features. "I never thought you would. I trust you, Shayla."

His gaze caught hers and locked. Her heart went into double time. Her pulse raced. An eternity in one glance.

Jeremiah banged the spoon on the tray of the high chair. Emily and the girls exchanged a look. Shayla blushed and pretended to be absorbed in her coffee.

Luke heaved a breath. "All right, then. I leave the farm in the hands of you extremely capable ladies."

Krista did a fist pump. "We are the mighty, mighty Morgans." In her stocking feet, she gyrated around the kitchen. "Say it with me now. We are the mighty, mighty—"

"Such a drama queen." Caroline rolled her eyes.

They all laughed. Even Mr. Stoic. And Shayla was glad to have lifted some of the shadows from his eyes. There was a mad dash for everyone to finish breakfast and get ready for day two of Open House weekend.

On his way out the door, he caught her alone in the kitchen, wiping down the high chair.

She refastened the tray. "We'll see you after closing tonight."

Luke shrugged into his coat. "What about the Christmas lights?"

She paused, the dishcloth in her hand. "I figured with you having to cover the tree lot..." She swallowed.

"If you'd rather not go with me, I understand."

She dropped the cloth on the tray and moved closer. "That's not it at all. But I thought with everything going on today, showing me the lights would be the last thing on your mind."

He stuffed his hands in his coat pockets. "Actually, despite everything going on today, showing you the Christmas lights is the *only* thing on my mind."

"Oh." She couldn't seem to tear her eyes from the vein pulsing in his jaw.

"So we're still on?"

At the hopeful note in his voice, she looked into his dark eyes.

"For our date?" He took his hands out of his coat pockets.

She nodded.

He smiled, the lines fanning out from the corners of his eyes. "Great. Until then." He double-tapped the door frame with his palms.

"Until then," she rasped.

Still smiling, he headed out.

The day at the farm went surprisingly well. Local folks were generous in helping her place the larger trees in the baler. At three o'clock, Emily declared Shayla's work done for the day.

"But…"

Emily put her arm around Shayla's shoulders. "We've made a great team, but now you and Jeremiah should go enjoy some time at the winter festival."

She looked around at the milling customers. "But what about—"

"We got this." Caroline gestured. "Only a few hours till dark and we close anyway."

"Luke's been texting Mom." Krista planted her hands on her hips. "Big bro is going to kill us if we don't send you to town ASAP."

"I don't feel right about leaving y'all."

"He asks so little of us." Caroline reached for her hand. "Please help us do this for him."

Luke's sisters were so much more than she'd initially credited them. And family so much more wonderfully complicated than she'd ever imagined. "Okay."

"Hoo-rah!" Krista raised her arm.

"If you're going to do that weird dance thing again," Caroline huffed, "I'm going to town with Shayla and Jeremiah."

Shayla frowned. "How am I supposed to get to town?"

"Take my car." Caroline handed her the keys to her red Toyota. "Luke installed the car seat before he left this morning."

So very thoughtful. So very Luke.

By four o'clock, she found herself on the winding mountain road to Truelove. There'd been a scramble to get Jeremiah and herself ready. She flicked a glance at herself in the rearview mirror.

She hoped she looked all right. She'd agonized over what to wear from her meager wardrobe. She settled on a soft blue sweater, which brought out the blue of her eyes.

In the back seat, Jeremiah contentedly gummed a set of plastic keys. His needs were so simple. Food. Clean diaper. Love.

Having been warned by Emily that Main Street would be closed to traffic today, she bypassed downtown and took a quick detour through the neighborhood where IdaLee lived to get to the other side of the square.

It appeared the entire population of Truelove had turned out for Santa on the Square. The sidewalks were jammed with festivalgoers. She pulled in behind the camper and parked beside his truck on the tree lot.

Finishing a sale with a customer, Luke smiled when he saw her. Seeing her favorite Christmas tree farmer, her heart did a pitter-patter. As soon as the customer left with a tree, he strolled over to where she and Jeremiah waited at the front of the camper.

"Hi," she breathed. Her breath fogged in the crisp mountain air.

Luke reached for her son. "Hi, yourself." Jeremiah went eagerly into his arms.

She patted the backpack slung over her shoulder. "I come bearing treats. Your mom sent along dinner."

He playfully tugged on Jeremiah's little fingers. "You're the treat. Dinner is a bonus."

"Better not let the matchmakers hear you talk like that."

"Let 'em hear." He nudged his chin at the baby, who was transfixed by the multicolored lights flashing from the giant snowman beside the camper.

Jeremiah bucked in his arms and gurgled.

She laughed. "I think he's trying to talk to it."

"I prefer talking to you." Luke gave her an admiring glance. "I like the blue sweater underneath your coat. Makes your eyes look even prettier."

"Thank you." She felt her cheeks warm. "But if you keep talking like that, you're going to completely turn my head. I had no idea you could be so charming."

"I had no idea, either." Looking sheepish, he repositioned the baby in his arms. "You must inspire me."

"Let me put the plates inside the camper." She climbed the camper steps. "I'll be right back."

Minutes later when she emerged, she spotted Sam Gibson crossing the street to the tree lot. He waved.

Luke gave him a thumbs-up and turned toward the square. "Coming, Shayla?"

Jeremiah twisted in his arms, keeping his eye on the dancing snowman. Sam warmed his hands over the fire in the barrel.

"Wait." She walked fast to keep pace with him. "Don't you need to help Sam?"

"Sam's going to finish my shift at the stand so Jeremiah can visit Santa. After the sun sets, we can view the Christmas lights." Luke took her arm as they crossed to the square. "You missed the parade, but Miss GeorgeAnne in her elf costume is worth the price of admission."

"Miss GeorgeAnne's wearing an elf costume?" Shayla sputtered. "Seriously?"

He grinned. "She takes her duty to Santa very seriously."

They wove their way through the crowd to the makeshift gazebo where Santa presided over Christmas dreams. There was a short line ahead of them with children eager to tell Santa their wish list. Piped through mounted loudspeakers, strains of "Winter Wonderland" floated on the air. Friends called greetings to Luke. No surprise, he was well-liked in town.

"Don't tell Jeremiah, but Santa's really Mayor Watson," he whispered in her ear.

"I won't tell." She shivered in awareness. "I promise."

The line slowly snaked its way forward. He was right about Miss GeorgeAnne in the elf costume. Quite a sight.

"Since we're trading true confessions—" she leaned into him "—I've always found Miss GeorgeAnne the most intimidating member of the Double Name Club."

"Don't we all." He drew his arm around her as a group of teenagers barged past. They found themselves backed against one of the three-foot plastic candy canes at the base of the gazebo steps. "But she's actually good with the kids who come to sit on Santa's lap."

Then it was their turn. From his bulbous, cherry-red nose to his snowy white beard, Mayor Watson was exactly as Santa should be. She placed her son in the mayor's arms.

"I feel sure you have been a good little boy this year." Gazing at the baby, Mayor Watson patted Jeremiah's orange-capped head. "What would you like Santa to bring you this year, young man?"

The infant's eyes widened. Alarm streaked across Jeremiah's countenance. His cheeks puffed. His mouth opened. And he shrieked bloody murder. His arms flailed, not in an attempt to reach his mother, but to get to Luke.

He caught hold of Jeremiah, who clung to him.

"Oh, Mayor." She went red. "I mean, Santa. I'm so sorry."

"No worries, my dear. It's not my first screaming baby." The mayor's pale blue eyes twinkled. "Nor shall he be my last, I fear."

As soon as he'd gone into Luke's strong arms, Jeremiah quieted.

What passed for a smile flitted across GeorgeAnne's thin lips. "I have a feeling everyone is getting what they hope for this Christmas." She handed Shayla a green-striped candy cane and beckoned to the next child in line.

Standing near the statue to the founder of True-love, Shayla shook her head. "That was awful."

"Terrible." He smirked. "Kara's serving free hot apple cider at the Jar. Why don't we walk over there and get some?"

"You better not be laughing, Luke Morgan." She tried to look stern. "That wasn't funny."

"I wouldn't dream of laughing." With Jeremiah solidly in his arms, he led the way across the square. "Absolutely not." He laughed.

She smacked his arm playfully. "It was embarrassing."

At the refreshment stand in front of the Mason Jar, a fortysomething blonde with a major addiction to tanning beds started jumping up and down. "Shayla! Shayla Coggins!" The waitress who'd become the café manager windmilled her arms. "Yoo-hoooo!"

Abruptly, he halted. "If you don't want to talk to Trudy—"

But she'd already allowed herself to be engulfed by Trudy. There were so few people in her life who'd ever actually been glad to see her.

"You taking good care of yourself, honey pie?" Trudy pulled away long enough to give Shayla a quick going-over and then hugged her again. "And I for sure want to get a gander at that sweet baby of yours, too."

Hip-swinging, gum-smacking Trudy gave her a brief rundown on the café, Leo the cook's love life and other grapevine news that had Shayla smiling.

Forking a piece of pie into his mouth, Zach kept Luke and Jeremiah company. Waving the fork at her, the lanky mechanic in his blue coveralls signaled he needed to talk when she was done with Trudy.

A frisson of unease wormed its way under her skin. Was there a problem? Had he discovered the car belonged to Wall?

Stepping out of the restaurant, chef and owner Kara MacKenzie joined them on the sidewalk.

"I'm going to let you and the boss catch up." Bubbly Trudy patted her shoulder. "Don't be a stranger, now, you hear?" She hugged Shayla again before moving to serve customers at the refreshment stand.

Kara smiled. "It's so good to see you, Shayla."

But Shayla's cheeks burned at the memory of their last conversation, when the photo had appeared in the newspaper after the tornado.

Desperate to make her escape before Wall came after her, she'd confessed her pregnancy to Kara and Trudy. And explained the trouble in which she found herself. Kara had insisted on giving her a two-week severance package. Unbeknown to Shayla, Trudy slipped an entire week's worth of tips into her handbag.

"I never meant to return to Truelove, Kara. I'm only passing through, but—"

Her former boss pulled her into a hug. "I've prayed for your safety every day. I'm happy you're back with people who love you." Kara's eyes, blue as blueberries, flitted toward the little boy in Luke's arms. "I want to meet your baby. I have a little boy of my own now."

Shayla smiled. "Is Maddox as cute as ever?"

Kara's mouth curved. "Takes after his father."

She squeezed her hand. "It makes me happy to see you so happy."

"Are you okay for cash? Can I—"

"I love you for offering." She blinked back moisture. "But I'm fine."

Kara understood the kind of poverty that had characterized Shayla's life. Before becoming an award-winning chef, Kara had spent much of her childhood in a homeless shelter.

Without meaning to, Shayla's gaze drifted toward Luke, deep in conversation with Zach. When her attention returned to Kara, the petite chef wore a knowing smile on her lips.

"Oh, it's like that, is it?"

"No, it's not like that." Shayla put her hand to her throat. "We're just friends."

"If you need anything—and I mean absolutely anything—don't hesitate to ask." The chef winked. "And there's always a slice of apple galette with your name on it in my café."

They talked for a few more minutes. It was getting late in the afternoon. The sky was streaked in shades of apricot, plum and orange. The festival was drawing to a close. The crowd on the square had thinned.

Kara excused herself to help Trudy dismantle the sidewalk stand. Shayla could no longer delay talking to Zach, and she found the guys in earnest conversation about who was the greatest race car driver of all time.

"Hey, Shayla." Zach dumped his paper plate into a receptacle. "I'm gonna need the title to the vehicle before I take the car apart to sell to the scrapyard. I looked in the usual places, but couldn't find it."

"Uh…oh…" She bit her lip. "I don't have it with me."

"I didn't expect you to have it on you this afternoon." Zach gave her a lazy grin. "That blue sweater sure does look pretty with your eyes."

"Thank you."

Luke scowled at his buddy.

"So, about the registration?" Zach scratched his

ear. "Technically, it should always be kept in the vehicle."

"I—I understand."

Despite her family's penchant for crime, it wasn't in her nature to lie. She racked her brain trying to come up with a plausible scenario to explain its absence. Anything to do with Wall was bound to lead to more uncomfortable questions.

"I'll have to look for it." She pulled at Luke's arm. "I'll get right on that."

Luke arched his brow at her.

"Weren't we going to look at the lights?" Catching his hand, she tugged him along the sidewalk toward the tree lot. "It's almost time for Jeremiah's supper. We're living on borrowed time."

In more ways than one. She didn't have a title to pass on to Zach. Therefore, she had to delay, distract and dodge the lanky mechanic until Monday morning when Luke dropped them off at the bus station. Then she'd be home free.

Or would she? She waited with Jeremiah beside the snowman as Luke stopped to give Sam a few closing instructions. For the first time since she had learned Wall was being released early, she reconsidered her plan to escape to Tennessee.

Would Nashville ever feel like home? In the dusky twilight, the strings of electric lights lining the perimeter of the square glowed. Luke laughed at something Sam said. A sharp, beautiful stab of longing lanced her heart.

Had perhaps she already found her true home?

Chapter Seven

❧

They drove around town in Caroline's Toyota, enjoying the displays of light and neighborhood decorations. Afterward, Luke followed her back to the farmhouse. He parked his truck in the driveway, allowing her to pull into the garage. He came up to her window. "Let me get Jeremiah out of the car."

She glanced over the seat at her son. "He's out like a light."

Going around the vehicle, Luke got in the car with her. "I'm in no hurry for our evening to end."

"Thank you for a wonderful evening." She smiled, in no more of a hurry than Luke. "It was such fun to see the lights reflected in Jeremiah's eyes. All that joy."

Luke leaned toward her. "I enjoyed seeing the same in yours."

Somehow she found herself a few inches closer to him, bridging the distance between them. They shared a look, a long look. And she wondered… hoped…prayed—

Krista flung open the door to the kitchen. "Hey, you two. How long are you going to sit out there?"

From the depths of the kitchen, Caroline groaned. "Are you clueless or just insensitive? Leave them alone!"

Krista opened her hands. "What did I do now?"

He scrubbed his face with his hand. "Sisters. Can't live with 'em."

Shayla laughed. "Can't live without 'em."

"Although I'd like to give it a try."

Getting out of the car, he unbuckled Jeremiah from the back seat. Luke carried him to the bedroom before heading downstairs again.

Not wanting to disturb her sleeping baby, she did a quick diaper check and laid him in his crib for the night. After turning on the monitor, she went downstairs and found the Morgans gathered around the kitchen island.

"Movie night." Krista grabbed a handful of popcorn from a large ceramic bowl and stuffed it into her mouth. "Hep yo'self."

Or at least that's what it sounded like to Shayla.

Emily handed her a smaller bowl. "I hope you'll come to church with us tomorrow. We have so much to be thankful for this year. Not the least of which is having you and Jeremiah with us to celebrate Thanksgiving."

Her insides did a flip-flop. Church meant facing people who knew her by her family's reputation. Yet how could she refuse? The Morgans had been so kind to her.

As usual, Luke said nothing. But he stopped eating popcorn. He tilted his head toward their conversation, his ear ever so slightly cocked as if he waited for her answer. Did he want her to come to church with them?

She found it impossible to resist the tug on her heart. "I'd love to. Thank you, Emily."

The next morning, birdsong awakened Shayla. She sighed. She'd been hoping for a sudden snowstorm. But the sweet sunshine of early morning poured through the lacy curtain, rendering her unable to come up with a single reason to beg off from going to church with the Morgans.

As she was learning, church, like most things with the Morgans, was a family affair. The women assured her church attire was mountain casual. She donned one of her nicer sweaters, which was wheat colored, and wore jeans, like Krista and Caroline. With Luke at the wheel, they all rode together in Emily's SUV.

Nestled in a glade on the edge of town, the steeple brushed a picture-perfect Blue Ridge sky. Despite the wintry chill, groups of congregants had gathered on the lawn in front of the steps of the white clapboard church.

Her stomach knotted. Carrying Jeremiah, she followed the Morgan clan across the small footbridge to the building. Clumps of snow dotted the creek bank. The rushing water tumbled over the moss-covered stones, creating a burbling melody.

Why had she ever agreed to come today? Because it would have been the height of rudeness to refuse to come to church with the family who'd taken her in and shown her such kindness, that's why.

Overnight, the temperatures had risen, a good sign that the pass over the mountains would be open. The bus line would be running again tomorrow morning. She just had to get through today.

Caroline and Krista broke away to chat with friends. Emily dragged her toward the group standing outside. "These things are best handled in a straightforward manner. Trust me."

She fought the urge to turn tail and run. She was only too aware of how she'd disappointed herself, the townspeople and God. This was a mistake. What was she doing here?

Perhaps sensing what she was feeling, Emily took firm hold of her arm, effectively trapping her in place between her side and Luke. "You remember Miss ErmaJean's grandson Ethan and his wife, Amber, don't you?"

"Yes, ma'am." She kept her eyes pinned to the

ground, dreading the condemnation she was sure to see on their faces. What must they think of her?

Emily tugged at her arm. "You've probably already met their little boy, Parker..."

She raised her gaze to the small child, bundled against the cold and held in his father's arms. The child must be about seven months old now. With his shock of curly blond hair, Parker Green resembled both parents. But unlike his twin half-sisters, Lucy and Stella, the baby had his father's distinctive gold-flecked hazel eyes.

Amber, a pediatric nurse, took her squirming son from her husband. "Born right after the tornado last spring."

Ethan laughed. "Not a day any of us are likely to forget anytime soon, baby cakes." He planted a quick kiss on his wife's cheek.

A bittersweet longing swirled through Shayla. She dared not glance at Luke as she tamped the feeling down, deep into the place she kept her dreams. But the couple's love for each other wasn't something she'd ever likely know firsthand for herself.

Cogginses didn't get happily-ever-afters.

Her arms tightened around Jeremiah. He might not have a daddy, but she'd do everything in her power to ensure he lacked for nothing else.

Amber shifted her baby son in the crook of her arm. "You were so heroic, Shayla, shepherding the children into the café cooler when the sirens went off that afternoon."

The tornado had descended while Truelove's youngest were in the middle of an Easter egg hunt in the town square.

She flushed. "I'm not... I wasn't..."

"Your baby's very cute."

The compassion she glimpsed in Amber's face surprised her. "Th-thank you."

Luke's mother had meandered over to the steps and appeared deep in conversation with the match-makers. But silent as a granite boulder, Luke remained at her side. Stuck like glue.

"I remember how hard it was to be a single mom." Amber touched a finger to Jeremiah's exposed cheek. "If you ever need to talk with someone who understands, I'm here for you."

"That's kind of you to offer." She blinked rapidly. "But I'm leaving town tomorrow."

Luke's brows bunched together.

Church bells chimed from the steeple.

"I'd better get Parker checked into the nursery." Amber tilted her head. "I can show you the way, Shayla."

Something akin to panic churned in her belly. "Jeremiah doesn't make much noise. Not yet. I can keep him with me during the service, can't I?" Her chest heaved. "Or is that a church rule?"

"Not a rule." Luke patted Jeremiah's head in

the orange knit cap. "He'll probably go to sleep. He can stay with us."

Jeremiah gave Luke a toothless grin.

Cupping her elbow in his palm, Luke steered her inside the sanctuary. Huge, hand-hewn beams soared above her head. Prisms of light shone through the stained glass windows.

Already seated, Emily waved and scooted over to make room for them on the pew. Luke's mother reached for Jeremiah. "Why don't I hold him, and you can enjoy yourself."

She unbuttoned her coat. What did people come to church to enjoy? She'd never been inside one before. No surprise, the Cogginses weren't church people. She knew as much about church as she did about God, which was practically nothing. But she desperately wanted to learn.

Her heart pounded. She removed Jeremiah's cap from his head as he lay contentedly in Emily's arms. She wasn't sure where Caroline and Krista had gone off to.

Shrugging out of her coat, she stole a surreptitious glance at Luke, seated next to her on the aisle. He looked handsome in a charcoal cable-knit sweater. His broad shoulders brushed the back of the pew.

Not sure what to expect from the service, she reckoned to keep quiet, fly under the radar and observe what others around her were doing. She didn't want to embarrass the Morgans.

Her breath hitched. Was that Mrs. Stewart, her old high school choir director, at the piano? Grayer, a bit more rounded, but yes, it was her old teacher. Mrs. Stewart placed her hands on the keys and began to play.

Lilting notes poured forth from the instrument. Shayla stilled, transfixed and captivated by the beautiful music.

Mrs. Stewart ended the piece with a flourish. Shayla felt sad it was over. But a man stepped to the podium and invited the congregation to stand.

Everyone rose, Shayla a half a tick behind. Luke cut his eyes at her. Out of her depth, she flushed, but she forgot her embarrassment when Mrs. Stewart began a new song on the piano.

The music leader called out a number for something to which Shayla had no clue. But she soon lost herself once again in the enjoyment of the music flowing around her.

With Emily bouncing Jeremiah in her arms, Luke reached into the wooden rack in front of them and removed a green-bound hymnal. Flipping a few pages, he held the book out to her and pointed to the second stanza. Shayla shot a quick look at the title—"Blessed Assurance."

Everyone sang together. Which reminded her of

the days singing in the high school chorale. The only place she'd fitted in as an awkward teen.

She listened for a split second to find her place and joined her voice to his. He had a nice, if slightly gravelly, baritone.

Mrs. Stewart had made sure no one left the choir without understanding how to read music. The older woman had been such an encouragement to her during those turbulent years. An anchor in the storm of her life.

All too quickly the song was over. They sat down. Luke placed a bulletin with the order of service on the pew cushion between them.

She made sure to keep a watchful eye on her son, should Emily tire of holding him. The music had lulled him to sleep.

Reverend Bryant—a kindly, scholarly man she remembered from waitressing at the café—stood at the pulpit. When everyone around her retrieved their Bibles, she was momentarily dismayed.

She did own a Bible—the one from the shelter. Why hadn't she thought to bring it? It was in her backpack at the Morgan farmhouse. Little good it did her there. She darted her eyes at Luke, whose Bible lay propped open across his knees.

He must have felt her glance because he inched over, erasing the space between them, to share his Bible with her. She was distracted by the tangy evergreen scent of pine and cedar that clung to his clothing. A pleasing scent.

Yet, despite his proximity and the thudding of her heart, she did somehow manage to pay proper attention to Reverend Bryant's thought-provoking message about preparing one's life for something called the beginning of Advent. The words from the Scripture soaked into her heart like rain on parched soil.

And as she rose for the final hymn, she congratulated herself on making it through her first church service without doing or saying anything to humiliate herself. Church hadn't been what she'd dreaded. Maybe when she and Jeremiah got settled in Nashville, they could find a place to worship there.

On the way out, lots of people stopped by to greet the Morgans. What was surprising was how many welcomed her, as well.

Mrs. Stewart caught her halfway down the aisle. "I hope you don't think I'm going to let you out of here without a hug first." Her old teacher's soft, lemony fragrance enfolded Shayla in a blanket of warm memories.

"I'm so glad you came today. It's been so long. Too long since I heard your lovely voice."

She was glad she'd come, too. She'd had no idea church was *this*—if she had, she'd have come long ago. "Your playing was wonderful." She hugged her teacher. "Just as I remembered."

Head peeking over Emily's shoulder, Jeremiah wiggled and grinned.

Mrs. Stewart smiled. "Is that your son?" In her clear blue eyes, no judgment. Only delight.

Shayla returned her smile. "Yes, this is Jeremiah."

Mrs. Stewart waved her hand toward Luke and his mom. "This young lady has the best voice it was ever my privilege to train. Do you still sing, Shayla?"

She swallowed. "Just to Jeremiah. But thank you, you're too kind." She dropped her gaze to the red carpet. "Life took me on a different path."

"Motherhood is no less worthy a path." Mrs. Stewart squeezed her arm. "I hope you sing to him often. Filling his heart with the beautiful sound of your voice."

She blushed at her praise. "I try, Mrs. Stewart."

An interesting expression flitted across the music teacher's austere features. "Did you see the announcement in the bulletin? I'm recruiting new choir members to join us for the upcoming Advent service. Would you join us?" She clasped her hands under her bony chin. "What glorious music we could make!"

Emily handed Jeremiah over to Caroline, who'd rejoined them. "That's exactly what I told her."

If Shayla had planned to stick around Truelove, she would've loved to become part of the choir. Then she remembered she was leaving. Tomorrow, actually.

No point in mooning over what would never happen. Could never happen. Not with the constant threat of Wall looming over her and Jeremiah. No point in dreaming, period.

"There's nothing I would enjoy more than singing with you again, Mrs. Stewart. But Jeremiah and I are headed out of town tomorrow."

Mrs. Stewart's face fell. "For how long?"

"For good, I'm afraid."

Luke scowled. "I'll be at the car." He shouldered past them.

She stared after him. What was with him? Just when she believed they'd achieved a friendship of sorts, he stalked off like that. She lifted her chin. Yet, when had a man ever proved worth the effort of friendship? Never, at least among the men that she knew.

Which proved how badly she needed a new start. And new friends.

"Luke probably has a million things to do at the farm."

Krista rolled her eyes. "Luke always has a million things to do at the farm."

Shayla had no desire to add to his troubles. She reached for her son. "It's been so wonderful to see you again, Mrs. Stewart, but I must say goodbye now."

Mrs. Stewart made her promise to keep in touch. "Never stop singing."

The knot in her stomach tightened. Despite her desire to pursue a career in the country music capital of the world, she didn't fool herself. The odds were against her success.

It could be a long, long time—if ever—before she'd get the opportunity to sing again for an audience of anyone but her son.

Standing in the driveway at the farmhouse late that afternoon, Luke waved goodbye one final time. Caroline and Krista's car disappeared around the curve of trees. He returned to the porch.

"It was great to spend time with them." Shayla shifted Jeremiah in her arms. "I always wanted sisters."

"Say the word and they're yours."

She rolled her eyes. "I know you're not serious. It's obvious how much you love them."

"Even when they're driving me nuts?"

"Yes." She laughed. "When will they be home again?"

"They have exams until the second week of December, and then they'll be back for the holidays." He rubbed his neck. "I guess you'll spend Christmas in Nashville?"

He wasn't sure why he phrased it as a question. A look clouded her eyes. Or was he reading too much into her expressive face?

She swallowed. "I suppose Jeremiah's first Christmas will be spent in Nashville."

The highway had reopened. The bus to Tennessee was running again. He knew because he'd checked. Come morning, he'd run her to the bus station at the county seat. And, most likely, never set eyes on her or Jeremiah again. His stomach tanked.

He stuffed his hands in the pockets of his coat. "I should…" His voice trailed away, and he made no move to go anywhere.

Was his family right? Maybe he did need a life of his own, just not now, though. Shayla didn't fit into the timing of his plan. Sure, there had been sparks between them. But the farm had to be his primary focus, not pursuing a long-distance relationship with her.

"You should…" Her mouth quirked. "Cut trees? Plant trees? What?"

His mom had already gone inside to lie down. After a nonstop weekend, all of them were exhausted.

A reluctant smile tugged at his lips. "On a farm, there's always something that needs doing."

"Let me put Jeremiah down for a nap." Her eyes

sparkled. "You should take advantage of my free labor while you can."

"I'll be in the shop."

There, he did a swift inventory of their remaining merchandise. Sales had been brisk over the weekend. With the part-timer at the tree lot out for the season, running the choose-and-cut business on the farm would have been nearly impossible without Shayla's help.

Luke was scrolling through the computer in the store when she strolled in with the baby monitor. "Down for the count?"

"Your sisters wore him out."

"My sisters wear everyone out." He frowned. "I should check on Mom. It's not like her to take a nap."

"Your mom was just getting up. She mentioned she might fix herself a cup of tea." Shayla tidied a shelf. "Did more wreath orders come in?"

He checked the computer screen. "Who knew that people in Ohio would want Fraser fir wreaths from our tiny farm in the Blue Ridge? Or people from Iowa. Or..." His gaze narrowed on the screen. "California."

She plumped the wreath's dangling red velveteen ribbon. "Apparently, Krista did."

"I give credit where credit is due." He scrolled through the orders. "Krista's little brainchild to increase revenue has really helped our bottom line over the last year."

"And Caroline created your website?"

Nodding, he jotted some notes on a pad next to the computer. "Her interest is more in marketing than the actual hands-on labor involved with the trees."

She freshened the wreaths on the lattice wall. "We each have our gifts."

He glanced at her again, but she was absorbed in rewiring a bunch of red nandina berries that had come loose from the grapevine frame.

This morning beside her at church, he'd been blown away by the power of her voice. He'd forgotten she'd been in the high school chorus with Mrs. Stewart. And her voice had only grown in maturity since then. Deep, rich. Full of multilayered color.

He'd enjoyed watching her face during the service. He'd been especially moved by her pleasure in the music. Seeing the familiar through her eyes. She had a way of bringing a sharp clarity to the life he too often took for granted.

She scanned the lattice wall. "We're running low on garland and swags."

We're.

Something as pleasurable as a sip of warm cocoa on a cold winter's day shot through him. He smiled. "Tomorrow I'll cut some more."

Her eyes brightened. "That sounds like fun."

She had the most extraordinary ability to make the ordinary seem like an adventure.

But then reality intruded. "You and Jeremiah will be on a bus by then."

"Right. Of course." Her face fell. "I forgot."

Luke only wished he could.

She drifted closer. Only the counter separated them. "Will this be your first season without Krista's help on the farm?"

He blew out a breath. He didn't like to think how his mom would handle choose-and-cut alone on the farm next weekend. "Farming involves a great deal of creative problem-solving."

"It takes a lot of smarts to be a farmer."

He rested his elbows on the wooden countertop. "Each day holds its own unique challenges."

She propped her elbows across from him. "You like that, don't you?"

To his surprise, he realized he did. "Being outdoors beats being cooped up in an office, hands down."

"What do you like about being outdoors?"

He'd found himself talking more over the last three days than he had in a month of Sundays. There was something encouraging about her. Like she wanted to hear what he had to say. Like she actually cared about knowing his thoughts.

"I like breathing the mountain air. Feeling the

warmth of the sun on my skin. Inhaling the tangy aroma of evergreen. Savoring the eye-popping color of spring wildflowers in the meadow."

"You paint such a word picture. I can see it in my mind." Reaching across the counter, she touched his hand. "You should write those ideas down, capture those feelings of the farm. It's a beautiful gift you have."

"Not much use to a tree farmer."

She shook her head. "You never know when it might prove a blessing to someone. You should share it. Send it in to a magazine. That's why we're given the gifts, you know." She tucked a strand of blond hair behind her ear and smiled. "To give back to others."

He'd never thought of his writing that way. As something to give to others. For the first time in a long time, the desire to write something—to put pen to paper, to string together words—welled inside him.

During the agonizing days of his father's final illness, writing had been a solace. An escape. A place to pour out his ragged feelings.

He'd jotted down one memory after another in story form. Of him and his dad working the farm together. But after his dad's death, and consumed by new responsibilities, he'd felt empty inside. Numb.

And he'd lost the will to write. The ability to

dream. The heart of creativity had left him. The gift had forsaken him. Gone forever, or so he'd believed.

Yet being with Shayla this week had ignited something deep within him. Something he'd long believed dead, brought to life again. By her.

Over the last few days in the early-morning hush, his favorite time on the farm, he'd found himself scribbling a few paragraphs on the back of a receipt from Allen's Hardware. An idea for a new story about the farm.

"Ba-ba-ba… Bah."

He and Shayla exchanged a quick, commiserating look. "Little man sounds wide-awake."

She sighed. "The naps are growing shorter."

Luke grinned. "He's afraid he's missing out on a Morgan family party."

"I'd better go check—"

"Jeremiah…" Emily's voice crooned through the monitor.

The baby babbled a chain of consonants.

Luke came around the counter. "He's starting to respond to his name."

"And not afraid to express his displeasure when his devoted servant, also known as Mommy, is a little too slow in feeding him."

Luke folded his arms across his plaid shirt. "When a guy needs his food, he needs his food."

She shook her finger at him. "Mommy isn't the only one jumping to do his bidding."

"My mom. Caroline." Luke unfurled his fingers one by one. "Krista."

"You."

"Me?" He made a show of widening his eyes. "I have no idea what you mean."

She cocked her head. "Your mother and sisters aren't the only ones spoiling him."

"In the immortal words of Miss ErmaJean, I quote, 'Enjoy your baby while you can. They're little such a short time.'"

Suddenly, he became aware of how close they stood to each other. And he battled the urge to put his arms around her. To draw her nearer. To touch her cheek.

To settle once and for all the overriding question of how silky the strands of her hair would feel running through his fingers.

He leaned down. Her lips parted. Their mouths almost but not quite touch—

Through the monitor, they heard something crash. His mother screamed. They sprang apart. The baby wailed.

"Jeremiah!" She dashed for the door. "I'm coming!"

"Mom!" he yelled.

And they ran toward the house.

Chapter Eight

Emily lay sprawled at the bottom of the stairs. Blood oozed from a small cut on her forehead.

Luke surged forward. "Mom!"

From the second story, Jeremiah continued to wail. Stepping carefully over Luke's mom, Shayla raced up the stairs.

Her heart in her throat, she hurried to the crib and did a quick visual survey. Arms and legs churning, her son lay on his back as she'd left him.

Jeremiah's face was brick red from crying. His eyes were squeezed shut, and tears dribbled down his downy cheeks. She scooped him into her arms.

Holding him against her shoulder, she patted his back. "Mama's here. Shh, it's okay." His little body shuddered with sobs. "What happened, honey?" Not for the first time, she wished he could tell her what was wrong. "What's got you scared?"

In the absence of apparent injury, after only a

handful of months she knew what the sound of each of his cries meant. This sharp droning cry wasn't anger or discomfort. It was a startled fear.

She carried him into the hall. "You're okay, sweetheart. Don't cry. You're safe."

Luke hovered over his mother. "Where does it hurt, Mom? Can you move your legs?"

Repositioning Jeremiah so he could see her face, Shayla picked her way carefully down to Luke. "Emily?"

"I'm so sorry." Luke's mom looked up from her awkward position on the floor. "I was going to get him a bottle from the kitchen." Her gaze appeared slightly dazed. "I remember feeling woozy, and the next thing I knew, I was tumbling."

Luke crouched next to his mother. "Try to sit up."

"I must've missed my footing." A single tear trekked across her cheek. "Getting old and clumsy, I guess. Is the baby all right?"

Shayla went cold at the thought of what could have happened if Emily had been carrying Jeremiah when she slipped. "You're not old or clumsy, Emily. Accidents happen." She willed her heart to settle. "When you fell, the clatter scared him, that's all. He'll be fine."

The sound of her voice was already soothing Jeremiah. His full-blown cries had lessened to whimpers.

Sitting up, Emily rested against the rail. She touched a hand to her head and winced. There was a smudge of blood on her fingertips.

Luke frowned. "You're going to need to go to the ER."

"But—"

"You could have a concussion." He took firm hold of her arm to pull her upright. "The cut may need stitches."

Putting weight on her right foot, Emily inhaled sharply. If it weren't for Luke's quick grab around her waist, she would have fallen again.

"No arguments, Mom. We'll take your car."

Her lips white with pain, she nodded. Assisted by her son, she hobbled toward the kitchen and the garage.

"Can we go with you?"

He glanced at Shayla. "You don't have to—"

"We love Emily, too. We want to make sure she's okay. Unless you think we'd be in the way." She swallowed.

Here she was butting herself and her child into their family business again.

"You and Jeremiah are never in the way." His mouth tugged at the corners. "Just so you know, though, there could be a long wait to get Mom checked out."

His dark eyes gleamed with an emotion Shayla

wasn't sure how to read. Friendship? Acceptance? Something more?

Before they were interrupted, had he really been about to kiss her in the shop?

She adjusted the baby on her hip. "We don't mind. We'll keep you company, won't we, Jeremiah?"

"Let me get Mom in the car." He reached for his mother's coat hanging on the peg inside the door. "You grab what you need for yourself and the baby."

Five minutes later, she entered the garage with her bundled son. Emily sat in the front with the passenger seat reclined. Good thing the car seat hadn't been removed from the SUV since this morning.

He held out his arms. "I'll strap Jeremiah into his seat."

She handed him her son. A mere four days ago he'd refused to say Jeremiah's name, much less hold him. "Didn't think you liked kids."

"Not all kids. Only this little guy." Luke ducked into the car, shielding Jeremiah's head, which was covered in his orange cap. "He's grown on me." He snapped the buckles in place and climbed out.

"Krista calls it 'The Jeremiah Effect.'" She handed Luke his coat. "Don't forget this."

"I did forget." He put on the coat. "Thanks."

Always taking care of others, too often he neglected to take care of himself.

She folded herself into the back seat. He held the door, waiting for her to fasten her seat belt.

"Can't say that I blame you." She smiled at him. "Who could resist my adorable son? Resistance is futile. His charms wore you down."

An interesting look crossed his features. "He isn't the only one." He closed the door with a soft click.

Or at least that was what she thought he said, but she couldn't be sure. Wishful thinking? She'd probably misheard.

Hadn't she?

Luke parked at the emergency room entrance, and Shayla jumped out. Her arm draped across Shayla's shoulders, his mother climbed out of the SUV.

He leaned across the seat. "I'll park and then come right inside with Jeremiah."

The glass double doors whooshed open. They half hopped, half staggered across the threshold.

He waited a moment until they were clear before he pulled out from the drop-off point and over to the parking lot.

Shutting off the engine, he sent a quick text to Sam, with a short explanation of what had happened, asking for prayer for his mother.

Luke released Jeremiah from his seat. The baby's blue eyes lit up. His arms waved, reaching for Luke. "Do you know me, little buddy? Or do you only want to be picked up?"

Either way, it did his heart good to hold the baby close to his chest. He took an unexpected comfort in the clean baby smell of him. Shayla was a good mother. Despite her limited resources, she took good care of her son. He was always clean and happy.

He grabbed Shayla's backpack and sped toward the emergency room. A dull ache throbbed behind his eyes. Seeing his mother lying at the foot of the stairs had terrified him.

In the reception area, he searched for his mom and Shayla. Spotting them, his gut tightened. His mother sat slumped in a wheelchair while Shayla filled out a batch of papers stuck in a clipboard.

He sank into the vinyl chair beside her. "What did the hospital staff say?"

She traded him the clipboard for her son. "The doctor will get to us as soon as he can." Propping the child against her, she nudged her chin at the papers. "I answered as many of the questions as I could."

His mom held out her hand to Jeremiah. His fist coiled around her finger. "I'm so sorry to have caused such a ruckus. To have dragged everyone over the mountain to the hospital in the snow."

"Don't worry about us." Shayla gave her a side hug. "You concentrate on feeling better."

Luke carried the completed paperwork to the receptionist at the desk.

Striding toward the exit with his head bent, a distinguished man in his late fifties wearing a white lab coat halted in front of them. "Emily? Emily Morgan?"

A slow smile transformed his mother's features. "Dr. Jernigan."

"We agreed you would call me Russell." He knelt beside Luke's mom. "What have you done to yourself?" He touched a finger to a strand of her hair, brushing it aside to examine the cut on her forehead.

"Oh, Russell, dear." His mom smiled. "I misjudged the stairs and took a tumble."

Russell, dear? Who was this guy? How did his mother know this man?

Luke stiffened. "I don't believe we've met. I'm Emily's son." He made a move to rise, but Shayla laid her hand on his arm, stopping him.

"Russell is the pediatrician in Truelove." His mother angled toward the doctor. "What're you doing at the hospital on a Sunday evening?"

"A young patient of mine decided to take a run down the slope behind his house on the lid of a trash can."

His mom took a quick, indrawn breath. "Oh, no. I hope he's all right."

"A contusion. Broken arm. Blessed to be no worse off than he is, considering his encounter with a tree. No sign of a head injury." Dr. Jernigan placed two fingers on the inside of his mother's wrist. "Your pulse is elevated."

The pediatrician's office had only been open a few years. Before that, townspeople had to travel over the mountain to the county seat for medical care for their children. Amber Green worked there but only part-time since her son was born last spring.

"Russell, dear…"

Luke gritted his teeth.

His mom fluttered her hand. "This is my son, Luke."

"The Christmas tree farmer." The doctor gave him a brief but appraising look before turning his attention again to Luke's mother. "I've heard a lot about you."

"Can't say the same," he growled.

Shayla cut Luke a warning glance. His mother introduced Shayla and Jeremiah.

The doc didn't take his gaze off Luke's mom. "Did you hit your head? Did you black out at any point?" He cradled her face between his palms, looking deeply into her eyes.

If it weren't for Shayla's gentle, restraining pressure on his arm, Luke would have pushed the man away. His hands clenched the armrests.

Not that the good doctor's touch bothered his mother in the least. If anything, her slightly wan expression had been replaced by something he could only describe as a kind of radiance. The look she turned on the doctor made Luke's heart thud painfully in his chest.

Blushing, his mother explained the circumstances leading to her fall. The dizziness. Missing her footing. No blackouts.

Dr. Jernigan rose. "I'll make sure you're attended to right away. I would've been headed back to Truelove an hour ago, except I got the call to check on another young patient who got into her mother's hidden stash of Christmas chocolate and ate the whole box in one sitting." His classically handsome features lifted. "I don't believe in coincidences."

His mom sighed, rather too happily to Luke's mind. "Neither do I."

Dr. Jernigan stuck his hands in his lab coat pockets. "The Lord works in mysterious ways." The tips of his ears going bright pink, he grinned at Luke's mother like a schoolboy.

"*Very* mysterious," Luke grunted.

Shayla shushed him. Not unlike how she did when Jeremiah was fussing. He glowered at her for a second before his gaze darted to his mom, who was giggling like a…

He fumed. He didn't know what his mother was giggling like. He'd never seen her like this.

Before he could mount another objection, Dr. Jernigan wheeled his mother through the double doors into triage.

Jeremiah reached out to Luke. At least someone appeared glad to see him. He took the baby from Shayla.

She unbuttoned her son's jacket and eased his little arms out of the sleeves. From the backpack at their feet, she handed Jeremiah a vinyl baby board book, which he proceeded to gum.

The baby on his lap, Luke scanned the crowded waiting room. "We could be here a long time."

"Not as long as we could've been." She removed the baby's knit cap. "Thanks to Dr. Jernigan."

He snorted. "Not a fan."

She tugged at one corner of the book Jeremiah chewed on. Not strongly enough to pull it free, but with just enough resistance to cause her son to tighten his mouthy grip. He grinned at her around the soft edges. Scrunching her eyes at the baby, she made a funny face.

Jeremiah did a gleeful, whole-body wiggle. Luke tightened his grip.

"You would've preferred your mom wait hours before she received treatment?"

"No." His mouth flattened. "But I think the

way the pediatrician mooned over her was entirely unprofessional."

"Dr. Jernigan was nothing but courteous. And a gentleman."

He jutted his jaw. "I'm glad Caroline and Krista weren't here to witness how our mother behaved."

"You need to lighten up. Your mom is still an attractive woman." Shayla sniffed. "There was nothing wrong with how she responded to Dr. Jernigan."

"Are you kidding me?" Outraged, he glared at her. "It was totally unbefitting the mother of three adult children. And my dad only in his grave nine years."

Laughing, she fell back against her chair. "Do you hear yourself?"

"I don't see what's so hilarious about my mom acting like she's lost her mind over an old guy."

"Old guy? Dr. Jernigan is a very handsome man in his prime."

Luke curled his lip. "If you like gray hair and wrinkles."

"You're being ridiculous. He's probably the same age as your mother."

Luke wagged his finger. "Which is too old to be cavorting around with a man—"

"Did you just use the word *cavorting*?" She snickered.

"Making cow eyes at each other, then." He grimaced. "In front of God, the county and impressionable youngsters."

"Speak for yourself, Luke Morgan. Jeremiah thought the doctor and your mother charming."

"You, too, I suppose." He scowled. "But what's not to like, right? Fancy car, fancy house. Successful practice. What do I know? I'm just a Christmas tree farmer."

Shayla twined her arm through the crook of his elbow. "You are far more than a mere Christmas tree farmer. Not that there is anything wrong in working with God's creations and bringing joy to countless Truelove families year after year."

His chin dropped, brushing the white blond peach fuzz on Jeremiah's head.

Shayla's stomach did a funny roll at the sight of him holding her child. Not that she could tell him that. He'd believe she'd lost her mind.

"Trust your mom's judgment." She squeezed his arm. "Trust God. Trust what He's doing."

Luke slumped against her. "That's the thing. I've got trust issues."

She rested her head—just for a second, of course—on his shoulder. "Don't we all?"

Feeling too comfortable to move, she decided to stay where she was. For the time being.

He sighed. "The bank loan's coming due. I find out tomorrow whether they'll give me an extension or not. With Mom out of commission for the fore-seeable future and my part-time help at the tree lot unavailable, maybe I should just admit defeat and throw in the towel this season."

The despair in his voice hit her hard. The hope-lessness. The sense of failure. She'd been there, for basically her entire life.

She lifted her head to check Jeremiah. Lying against Luke's chest, he'd drifted to sleep. Luke had closed his eyes, too. But she knew he wasn't sleeping.

By his pinched brow and tight mouth, she guessed worrisome thoughts ricocheted around in his head like balls in a pinball machine. It gut-ted her to see him so distraught, so torn apart by the pressure and stress.

If only she could help him. Wait. Why couldn't she stay and help him? Relieve him of some of the burden, if at least temporarily.

But what about Wall?

After the photo appeared in the newspaper, she'd fled out of an abundance of caution. But Wall never actually sent anyone to Truelove. He didn't know about the part of her life in the dark cove on the other side of the mountain. He knew nothing of her ties to the area.

Even if he'd seen the photo, he'd never guess in a million years she'd return to Truelove. Why not hang around Truelove until Christmas? Why not hide from Wall here?

Tentacles of fear strangled her heart. She couldn't—shouldn't—stay in Truelove. She couldn't take the chance on Wall finding her. Or could she? She sat up.

Luke opened his eyes. "What is it?"

The Morgans had done so much for her. Why not return the favor? For once in her life to not be the object of charity but, instead, the giver of it. The notion appealed to something deeply broken inside her.

"I want to stay with you," she blurted before she could talk herself out of it.

His hand on Jeremiah, he eased upright. "What're you talking about?"

That hadn't come out quite the way she'd intended. "I can help your mom get back on her feet and, on the weekends, cover the choose-and-cut customers while you handle the tree lot in town."

"I appreciate you wanting to help us." He rubbed his forehead. "But there's no way you can physically manage everything at the farm on your own."

She squared her shoulders. "We'll make it work. We'll find a way."

He shook his head. "I can't ask you to sacrifice—"

"You're not asking. I'm offering."

"But what about Nashville?"

She tossed her hair over her shoulder. "Nashville will be there in January the same as in December." She tucked a strand of dangling hair behind her ear.

A beat thrummed in the hollow of his throat. "I don't want to derail your plans."

"Not derail. Postpone." She touched his sleeve. "I can't leave you to handle the entire season and your mother alone. And if you can afford to pay me what you were planning to give the part-timer at the tree lot, I can earn some money to give us a little cushion when we arrive in Nashville."

"Sure, I can do that." His mouth turned down. "But—"

"It will be Jeremiah's first Christmas." She opened her palms. "What better place to celebrate his first Christmas than on a Christmas tree farm with people we—he—loves?"

Her gaze flicked to Luke, but he didn't seem to have noticed her slip of the tongue. She'd said "we," but she'd meant "he" as in Jeremiah, of course.

Because how utterly ridiculous would it be for someone like her to fall in love with Luke Morgan?

"I could also join the Christmas choir and work with Mrs. Stewart again. The voice is like a muscle." She warmed to her theme. "As with any athlete, it must be exercised and trained for the best results. Good preparation for Nashville auditions."

Why not give Jeremiah a wonderful first Christmas? A real family Christmas, the likes of which she might never be able to offer him again. The kind she'd never experienced but always longed for.

"There's still the issue of manpower on the choose-and-cut weekends."

"People would be glad to help you if you—"

Luke grimaced. "I can't ask."

Her eyes narrowed. "You mean you *won't*. That stubborn pride of yours."

"I refuse to put myself or the farm deeper in debt. Even with friends." His mouth thinned. "Not when there's no chance I can repay them."

She took a breath. She so didn't want to go there with him, but if that was the only way to make him see sense...

"Then based on that reasoning you practically owe *me* the chance to repay my debt to *you* for that other thing."

Chapter Nine

Unsure what she meant, Luke cocked his head. "What other thing?"

"I owe you for the Snack Pak."

His brow furrowed. "Excuse me?"

"Soft drink, hamburger, small order of fries and a toy."

Luke got the distinct feeling somehow she'd turned the tables on him, that he'd been outmaneuvered by his own logic.

"I know what the Burger Depot Snack Pak is, but what does that have to do with you owing me?"

"Autumn of my freshman year. You were a senior." She gulped. "It was the cheapest thing I could find on the menu," she whispered.

He stared at her blankly.

"Away game." She fluttered her hand. "Big football rivalry."

He gave a slow nod. "I was the team manager."

"I collected glass bottles for weeks to redeem so I could afford the ticket." She let out a small trickle of breath from between her lips. "In chorus, Mrs. Stewart asked me to represent our high school in a duet of the national anthem before kickoff. It was the first time someone saw anything special about me. It was an honor to be asked. I couldn't say no."

He smiled. "I remember everyone asking who the little freshman with the big voice was. Everybody saw how special you were that night."

She knotted her hands in her lap. "I rode the bus with the team, the cheerleaders and the band. I had never been to a football game before."

"Great game." He shifted positions as Jeremiah snuggled into him. "One of Sam's all-star quarterback performances. We won."

She moistened her lips. "But I didn't realize after a victory, the bus always stopped at the Burger Depot for an after-game celebration."

He shrugged. "I still don't—"

"I had only saved enough for the ticket." She looked him square in the face. "I didn't have enough money to eat at the Burger Depot."

His gut tightened.

She fretted the edge of her sweater. "The bus was locked. Everyone was so happy, standing in line waiting to order. Except me. Everyone chatted with their friends. Except for me. I had no friends. People whispered. Pointed at me standing by the door."

Reaching over the baby, he took her hand.

"That's when it hit me how much I hated being poor. Never belonging. And I knew—" She ground her teeth. "I just knew it would always be that way. I'd always be nothing more than that trashy Coggins girl."

It hurt him on an almost a visceral level to hear her demean herself. "Shayla, you're not—"

"So do you know what I did with that profound realization?" Her eyes blazed. "With my life laid out before me in the cold, public clarity at the Burger Depot?"

He twined his fingers through hers.

"I cried." She lifted her chin. "I stood there and cried."

High school was hard. Tougher for some than others. He felt it for her like a punch in the gut. The crushing despair she must've experienced. The humiliation of being different, of not fitting in. The utter hopelessness of her situation.

She would have withdrawn her hand from his, but he held on. Refusing to let go, wishing he could somehow exchange his strength for her remembered pain. She might have been alone that night in high school, but she wasn't alone now.

"It was one of the lowest moments of my life.

Not the first." Her beautiful eyes drifted to the child he held in his lap. "And it wouldn't be the last."

Not the last… He was bothered as much by what she didn't say as what she did. A wave of protectiveness washed over him.

She dragged her gaze off her son. "Do you recall what you did that night at the Burger Depot?"

His mouth went dry as sudden memory of a long-ago evening flooded through his brain.

"You walked right up to me." She shook her head, a hint of bemusement on her sweet features. "And told me you were going to buy my dinner." Tears welled in her eyes. "I still don't know why you did that. Nobody else even bothered."

He swallowed past the boulder in his throat. "I—I couldn't bear to see you standing there crying."

"It remains the loveliest thing anyone has ever done for me." Her eyes grew distant. "I wasn't used to it, you see."

"Used to what?"

Her eyes flicked to him. "Kindness."

Something tore at his heart.

"And now that I've met your family, I see you are a testament to your raising." Her eyes went half-mast. "As I am to mine."

"Shayla…"

"But I aim to do better by my son." Her blue eyes sparked fire. "I will do better by Jeremiah."

"You don't owe me anything, Shayla."

The last thing he wanted from her was to feel beholden to him. Or feel a sense of misplaced gratitude for a long-ago act of decency. What he wanted her to feel for him was—

His heart pounded against his ribs. What did he want from her?

"Let me do this for you, Luke." She bit her lip. "Please."

Her shame at finding herself dependent upon others was palpable. How hard-won was self-respect for a woman of her background. He was on the edge of losing his heritage and his livelihood. He *did* need her help with the farm and his mom. So why not let her?

"There's still the issue of the cutting and baling on the weekends."

"We'll figure something out, Luke."

And when she gazed at him like that with those big, blue eyes of hers…he had a hard time remembering his name, much less refusing her anything. Especially when her offer was so selfless.

He'd be an idiot to refuse. As an added bonus, he'd get to enjoy being with her and Jeremiah for a few more weeks. A gift he'd be stupid to reject.

For reasons he preferred not to examine too closely, he accepted and stuck out his hand. "Thank you."

"It's a win-win for us both." She shook his hand. "We'll be helping each other. It's what friends do."

But suddenly friendship didn't seem nearly enough. Not when it came to Shayla.

Several hours later, Dr. Jernigan returned, pushing Emily in the wheelchair through the double doors into the reception area. Shayla took her sleeping child from Luke.

"Mom?"

"I'm fine." His mother waved her hand. "But feeling foolish."

Dr. Jernigan squeezed her shoulder. "Not foolish."

Crossing his arms, Luke widened his stance. "What's the diagnosis? Why did she fall?"

Eyes flickering to Luke's mom, Dr. Jernigan hesitated.

Reaching up, his mother patted the doctor's hand. "It's okay to tell him, Russell. He's my son. I've nothing to hide."

Luke blanched. "It's serious, then?"

The pediatrician stuck his hands in the pockets of his white coat. "Nothing rest won't cure. She's not taken her blood pressure medication for a while."

His mom flushed. "The girls came home. We got busy with the farm. The last few days I simply forgot."

Shifting Jeremiah, Shayla stood up beside Luke. "That's why Emily was dizzy?"

Dr. Jernigan nodded. "Apparently, she hasn't felt well all weekend."

"I knew she seemed more tired than usual." Luke dropped to a crouch beside his mother. "Why didn't you say something? If I'd known—"

"This isn't your fault, son." His mother took his hand. "I didn't tell you because I didn't want to add to your worries."

Luke surveyed the white bandage on her forehead and the heavily wrapped dressing taped around her ankle, peeking out from below the hem of her jeans. "How badly did she injure herself in the fall?"

"The attending physician in the ER ran the usual precautionary tests. Emily sustained a bad sprain, but thankfully nothing more serious." Jernigan pushed his wire-rimmed glasses higher onto the bridge of his nose. "And despite her assurances to be on her best behavior, I know Emily will need your help to ensure she sticks to her promise to stay off that foot as much as possible to allow the ankle time to heal properly."

Luke jutted his jaw. "You can count on us, Doc. From this minute forward, Emily Morgan is a woman of leisure."

"This is our busy season." His mother frowned. "You need me."

"I'll always need you, Mom. But Shayla is going to stay at the farm with us until after Christmas." He rose to his full height. "We've got everything covered."

"That's right." Shayla smiled. "You concentrate on your recovery. Luke and I will handle Christmas at the farm."

"Excellent." Dr. Jernigan placed his hand once more on Luke's mother's shoulder. "I'll stop by tomorrow to check on you."

"I can't tell you how much I'll look forward to that, Russell."

"Didn't realize doctors still made house calls..." Luke muttered.

Shayla aimed a well-placed elbow to his ribs. He glared at her. She gave him a pointed look.

"Uh, I mean, thank you." Shifting ever so slightly out of elbow range, Luke extended his hand to the doctor. "Thank you for taking good care of my mom, Dr. Jernigan."

The pediatrician insisted on waiting with Emily and Shayla while Luke went to retrieve the SUV from the parking deck. After transitioning to the front passenger seat, Emily waved at the doctor as Luke drove away.

In the back seat with Jeremiah, Shayla clicked her seat belt in place. "Dr. Jernigan seems like a nice man."

Emily angled around. "Isn't he, though?" Her eyes darted to Luke. "What did you think, son?"

"I think…" He kept his eyes on the road. "He's certainly very attentive. And…"

"And?" His mom prompted.

Shayla held her breath.

"Maybe we could have him over for dinner later this week." His gaze sought hers in the rearview mirror. "If Shayla doesn't mind cooking for one more."

She shot him a brilliant smile. "I don't mind."

It was after nine o'clock before they reached the farmhouse. Luke carried the still-sleeping Jeremiah from the car to his crib. A small lamp on a table at the top of the landing cast a dim glow.

She helped Emily hobble up the stairs to her room. Maintaining she was fit enough to get herself to bed unassisted, Emily bade her good-night.

Shayla ventured farther down the hall to her own bedroom. At the same moment she reached for the doorknob to check on Jeremiah, Luke opened the door and stepped out. He shut the door softly behind him.

Suddenly, she became aware of how quiet the farmhouse was on this late-November evening. And how close she stood to Luke. Her heart did a treacherous uptick.

He was tall. She had to lift her head to get a good look at him. Like many of the mountain boys she'd grown up with, he was broad-shouldered. But unlike them, he was also disturbingly good-looking.

Shayla's heartbeat accelerated. Only he wasn't a boy anymore. He was a man. An extremely attractive man—made even more so by his unawareness of his own appeal.

He nudged his head at the closed door. "Jeremiah is such a trouper."

Was she the only one finding it hard to breathe? She really needed to get a grip on her runaway emotions. Luke was her friend and, at least temporarily, her employer.

The atmosphere between them needed lightening so she grinned at him. "Like his mom, you mean?"

"Yes." He brushed his lips against the top of her head. "Exactly like his mom," he whispered.

Her heart sang.

"I should say good-night." He raked his hand over his head. "Between the farm and Jeremiah, we'll have an early start."

She reached for the doorknob. "Good night."

He gave her a lopsided smile that stole her breath. "Sweet dreams, Shayla."

Ducking into the darkened room, she shut the door behind her. Pressing her shoulder blades against the wood, she let her head fall back. Was something really developing between her and

Luke? Good things didn't usually happen for her. *Is this Your doing, Lord?*

As for her dreams? Sweet dreams, for sure. Because she had a sneaking suspicion, she'd be dreaming of Luke.

Instead of heading to bed, Luke went downstairs to check that the doors were bolted for the night. He was surprised to find the door to his office ajar. His laptop was open.

He sank into the chair and tapped the keyboard. A bluish glow lit the darkened room. The screen sprang to life, revealing an open document.

Strange. He didn't remember opening the short story he'd written about his dad, much less leaving it on the screen. The cursor blinked at him.

He clicked the file closed and powered down the computer. He leafed through the file folder on his desk to make sure he had the information he'd need when he met with the loan officer at the bank tomorrow.

Everything depended on the bank's verdict. And if they decided not to extend the loan? That was an outcome that didn't bear thinking about.

Overcome with weariness, he rested his elbows on the desk and dropped his head into his hands.

He much preferred to think about Shayla. Upstairs, he'd been so close to kissing her. But at the last minute, he'd talked himself out of it.

She wasn't sticking around permanently. There was no point in getting attached. He already felt far too much of a bond with Jeremiah than he'd ever anticipated.

And if he lost the farm? What then? In a few, short weeks, Shayla would have a new life in Nashville. Yet, his life was here. He'd never envisioned himself somewhere else. If not on the farm, then somewhere close by. The mountains and Truelove were as essential to his well-being as oxygen in his lungs.

"Please, God," he whispered. "Help me to find favor with the bank."

That night, between worrying over the bank's decision and the quagmire of his feelings for Shayla, sleep proved elusive. The next morning he awoke to find her making breakfast in the kitchen. In his high chair, chubby, adorable Jeremiah gummed a rubber spatula.

"Sit down and eat." She poured coffee into a mug and handed it to him. "What time's your meeting at the bank?"

He pulled out the chair next to the baby. Jeremiah lost his grip on the spatula, and it fell to the floor.

Setting the mug on the table, Luke leaned over to retrieve the spatula for the little boy. "Later this morning."

"Nice tie." Flashing him a smile, she set a plate

of pancakes in front of him. "No offense, but you clean up pretty well for a tree farmer."

He laughed. "None taken. And thank you." He raised his eyebrows. "I think."

Gripping the spatula once more, Jeremiah grinned at him. Opening his fingers, he let go of it. Head craned over the side of the tray, he watched the spatula fall.

Bending, Luke scooped it off the floor. He handed it to Jeremiah, who promptly dropped it over the side again. The baby burbled.

"Dude!" Luke cut his eyes at Shayla.

She smirked. "You realize you're his new favorite game this morning, don't you?"

Luke leaned down.

"You're going to get tired of this game long before he does."

"I don't mind." Straightening, he handed the spatula to the child. "He's a great kid." He placed his palm on Jeremiah's short, silky fuzz-ball head. "What're your plans for the day?"

She took a sip of coffee. "I'll help your mom get dressed and do whatever else needs to be done in the house or the store to get ready for next weekend."

He sighed. "If I haven't said it before, I want you to know how much I appreciate—"

"Eat your pancakes before they get cold." She smiled over the rim of her mug.

"Only if you promise me you'll call Mrs. Stewart and tell her you're joining the Christmas choir on Wednesday night."

"Maybe I shouldn't." She bit her lip. "There's so much to do…your mom…the farm…"

"They'll both be fine for a few hours while you attend choir practice."

Later that morning, after his appointment with the loan officer, he returned to the house to change into his usual farm attire before heading back to town to open the tree lot that afternoon.

The meeting had gone well. He felt good about how he'd laid out his case. The bank officer had appeared open to an extension. Shayla met him inside the door of the farmhouse. They moved into the living room.

"It's in God's hands now." He took a deep breath. "This trust thing is hard."

"Tell me about it." She touched his arm. "I'm praying for the future of the farm."

"We'll all be praying." Resting on the sofa, his mother nodded. "In the palm of His hand is the safest place for any of us to be."

The next few days passed in a delicious, heartwarming blur. Shayla and Jeremiah settled into a routine. A true friend, Sam had telegraphed Luke's seasonal dilemma to all and sundry on the Truelove grapevine.

People came out of the woodwork to help Luke man the tree lot. His buddies at the firehouse took it upon themselves to organize a rotation of volunteers, and the Double Name Club flew into action. Miss ErmaJean and her friend Bill, the retired school administrator, even claimed a shift or two. Kara insisted on providing meals for the family each evening.

It was just one more indication of how seriously Truelove took its neighborliness. Good people. A good town.

Shayla was having second and third thoughts about leaving. Yet she and Jeremiah couldn't impose on the Morgans' hospitality forever.

On Wednesday evening, choir practice was everything she could have hoped for and more. It was so wonderful to be under Mrs. Stewart's tutelage again. The music transported Shayla to her happy place.

Afterward she lingered a few moments in the rehearsal room to help Mrs. Stewart sort new music into the proper cubbyhole. Each choir member had their name on the open-faced shelving lining the far wall. Seeing her own name alongside the others, she couldn't deny the thrill of pleasure that rippled through her.

Solid and real. Like she belonged here. Like this was her home.

"I could really use your expertise with directing the children's choir on Thursday evenings."

She handed her teacher another black folder. "Me?"

"You'd be a natural with them." Mrs. Stewart tucked the leather folder into the correct slot. "What with coordinating the adult choir, the musicians and a ton of other details, I'd be so grateful to have someone of your caliber on board."

Someone of her caliber? A lump formed in her throat.

"It sounds like something I'd love to do." Shayla knotted her hands. "But there's Jeremiah. I can't ask Luke to watch him two nights in a row."

"Talk to him before you refuse." Mrs. Stewart patted her hand. "Trust him. Trust yourself."

Mrs. Stewart was the best kind of teacher. She'd been God's gift to Shayla during those bleak growing-up years. Believing in her talent. Giving her the confidence to dream for herself. Yet at the same time, she'd always challenged Shayla to stretch herself musically and to reach for more.

Emily got stronger every day. Dr. Jernigan made it a point to stop by every evening on his way home from the office.

"It's not exactly on his way," Luke growled Thursday night after dinner.

Shayla handed him a plate to dry. Emily had retired for the night.

"I haven't seen my mom so happy since Dad..." Frowning, Luke concentrated on drying the plate. Rubbing the same spot over and over. "But if she's happy, I guess I can be happy, too."

"Good to know you've decided Dr. Jernigan is not quite the threat to society you imagined him to be." Shayla removed the plate from his hands before he broke it. "Progress. I love it."

"I love—" He grabbed a bundle of silverware from the drain board. "I'll put this in the drawer."

What she would give to know what he'd been about to say before his natural reticence kicked in. How did Luke feel about her?

He must hold her in some regard because he'd let her read many of the stories he'd penned about life on the farm. He was so talented. And she'd told him so.

The weekend was busy with Luke in town at the tree lot. But Shayla was in no way left alone to cope with choose-and-cut on the farm. Lila and Sam brought Miss IdaLee, who immediately positioned herself at the register inside the store. Maggie Hollingsworth arrived next.

Shayla was glad Chief Hollingsworth hadn't come to help, though. He seemed like a nice guy, but because of her family's history, law enforcement made her nervous.

Unexpectedly, as the most seasoned Morgan

Farm employee on-site, she found herself supervising the others.

Midday, AnnaBeth and Jonas arrived, and a stooped, elderly man also got out of their car.

As the trio walked toward the store, Lila got jittery. "Excuse me while I bring Aunt IdaLee out here, y'all." She flashed her husband, Sam, a panicked look. "This could end in disaster, or be the greatest thing since..." She wrung her hands.

He planted a kiss on his wife's brow. "Since beautiful, impossibly curly, red hair."

Throwing him a quick smile, she headed inside.

"Dare I ask what's going on?" Shayla ventured.

"The Double Name Club aren't the only ones matchmaking this Christmas." Sam folded his arms across his chest. "It's a match sixty-odd years in the making. Lila and AnnaBeth tracked down Aunt IdaLee's girlhood love, Charles Redfern. There was a misunderstanding, and as Aunt IdaLee explains it, they lost each other."

Lila emerged onto the porch with the old woman.

IdaLee fluttered her hands. "I was in the middle of a—"

The crowd in the yard parted. Charles Redfern stepped forward. "Ida."

Shayla held her breath and clasped her hands under her chin. She didn't know if second chances were possible. But, oh, how she hoped for the old woman's sake, as well as her own, that they were.

Taking a step forward, IdaLee tilted her head. Puzzlement was written across her features. Then she inhaled sharply. As recognition dawned, her hand flew to her throat.

"Charles?" She said his name with a dragged-out drawl, the one syllable becoming two.

The older man came to the foot of the steps. "It's me, Idaho."

Her cheeks turned a becoming shade of pink. "First meal I ever fixed him was mashed potatoes. When he was on leave during the Korean War."

"Still my favorite meal." Charles Redfern looked at her. "I never forgot you."

Miss IdaLee gripped Lila's arm. "I never forgot you, either."

"I know I look different than how you remember me." He removed the winter hat covering his balding head. "But you, dearest IdaLee, haven't changed a bit."

"Shameless flatterer," the older woman murmured.

But Shayla could tell from the curve of her lips that IdaLee was pleased.

Charles Redfern gazed at her. "The years have passed. But my feelings for you haven't."

"Nor mine for you, Charles." Coming down the steps, she gave her hand to him. And that was all it took. Shayla had never seen IdaLee so happy. The gathered crowd cheered.

Soon after, AnnaBeth drove the matchmaker and her reunited beau to the Mason Jar to continue their conversation over lunch. Shayla couldn't wait to fill Luke in on what he'd missed.

If the look in IdaLee's eyes for Charles was an indicator of true love… *Wow.*

Thinking of Luke, she sighed. What did she feel for him? She'd been wrong before, so terribly wrong.

Was it possible to fall in love over the course of a week?

Although, in truth, she'd been half in love with Luke Morgan since she was a girl. Yet this time, she knew her love for him was the real thing. The kind people wrote love songs about.

Could there be a second chance for her? For the first time, she felt such hope. Was true love possible?

Please, God. Let it be true.

Chapter Ten

On Sunday evening after shutting down the choose-and-cut operation for the weekend, Luke invited Shayla to go into town with him to meet Lila and Sam for the tree lighting in the square.

His mom, aided by Russell Jernigan, attempted to convince Shayla to leave the baby with them so he wouldn't miss his bedtime. But like whenever anyone tried to do her a favor, Shayla voiced her usual objections.

She didn't want to impose… Emily should be resting, not babysitting…

"For the love of a Christmas tree." Luke handed Shayla her coat. "Russell's a pediatrician. I think my mom and Jeremiah will be in good hands for one night without us."

Sitting beside her in the pickup truck on the way to town, he fiddled with a dial on the console.

"The heat in this old truck doesn't work as well

as it used to. Feeling cold over here by myself." He swept his hand across the space between them in the cab. "Might be a good idea for you to slide closer to me so we can consolidate the heat."

Her mouth quirked. "You think so?"

"Yep." He gave her an endearing grin. "I definitely think so."

Chuckling, she scooted next to him. "So let me get this straight." Her coat brushed against the hard muscle of his shoulder. "Last December, Sam went to an out-of-town wedding as Lila's plus-one, but when they returned in time for the tree lighting, everyone believed they were engaged."

"Only in Truelove." He laughed. "A pretend engagement led to a real engagement and, eventually, a late-spring wedding at AnnaBeth's FieldStone Dude Ranch."

"I get why the tree lighting is a big deal for them." She smiled. "A sweet, first anniversary of sorts."

Unbidden images sprang to his mind of making those kinds of traditions with Shayla. But would Shayla and Jeremiah still be in Truelove next December? Would he?

Putting his worries aside for the evening, he determined to make this night a special memory for both of them. It turned out to be fun. Lila had never been one of those stuck-up girls in high school. And although Shayla was younger than his friends by several years, Lila went out of her way to make her feel included.

Shayla's eyes sparkled when Mayor Watson flipped the lights for the trees. She seemed the most relaxed and happy Luke had ever seen her. He was glad he'd worked up enough courage to ask her to go with him.

Unlike Sam, he hadn't gone out with many girls. Asking Shayla to go with him to the Christmas lights and now the tree lighting had been a big deal. He hoped she understood without him having to say the words out loud how big a deal it was for him.

But that was as far as he was willing to acknowledge his feelings for the petite single mom. Plenty of time for them to get to know each other better. No need to rush the relationship. When the loan extension came through, the farm would be secure. And with the Christmas tree season soon to be over, he'd have more time for his writing. As for Shayla?

What was Miss IdaLee's old-fashioned phrase? *Woo.* That was it. He'd take his time and woo Shayla Coggins properly.

He could tell Truelove was working its unique charm on her. Maybe she'd decide to stay. And because it's what writers did, he could already envision a cozy future on the farm with her one day. Kara would offer her a job at the café again in a heartbeat. Shayla could sing in the church choir. He looked at her, laughing at something Sam had said.

She could say what she wanted about sturdy plow horses. Slow and steady did win the race—and the girl. Plodding had worked well for him his entire life. No reason wooing should be any different.

He exhaled. Glad to have worked that out in his head to his satisfaction. Soon after, Lila and Sam said good-night.

Later, after relieving one of his firefighter buddies manning the tree lot, Luke and Shayla warmed themselves by the fire barrel at the tree stand. "We probably won't get any additional customers tonight."

Holding her hands over the heat of the fire, she nodded.

"I could probably close for the evening." Not for the first time, he wished some of Sam's ease with the ladies had rubbed off on him. "But I'm in no rush to return to the farmhouse. Unless you are." He cut a look at her.

"Not at all." Bathed in firelight, her features glowed with a beauty that made his heart skip a beat. "This is wonderful." She smiled at him.

"Good."

Inwardly he groaned. Could he *be* more tongue-tied? For once why couldn't the words that flowed from his fingertips on the keyboard flow from his lips just as easily?

He tried again. "Kind of romantic, too, don't you think? Under the stars?"

"Definitely." She smiled. "Your words always paint such a vivid picture in my mind."

Pleased, he went on. "I figure you don't get many evenings off from Jeremiah. Gotta enjoy it while you can."

Her smile faded. What he'd meant to say was he didn't get to spend many evenings exclusively with her. Alone. But then that sounded like he didn't want Jeremiah around. Which was the furthest thing from the truth.

Luke rubbed his neck. "That didn't come out the way I intended. I adore the little guy."

"And he adores you." Her gaze fell to the orange-red blaze of the fire. "Neither you nor your family has ever pressured me to explain about Jeremiah's father."

"You don't owe any of us an explanation."

"I know, but I want to." Her eyes locked onto his. "After high school, all I could think to do was to get away from my family. I got as far as Greensboro. Got a job as a cashier at a discount store. I didn't understand about God then. I was lonely and desperate to be loved."

He shifted, not sure he wanted to hear the rest. But she'd listened to him as he poured out his grief over losing his father, the struggle to save the farm and his stifled creativity. He owed her the respect of returning the favor. No matter how uncomfortable he was at the idea of her relationship with Jeremiah's father.

"I made a lot of mistakes." Her eyes flashed. "But despite everything, I don't count Jeremiah as one of them."

Luke folded his arms across his coat. "As well you shouldn't. He's a gift."

"Beauty from ashes. I read that somewhere in the Bible the other day." She squared her shoulders. "I did things I'm not proud of. But some things can't be undone." Her face became stricken. "I'm so afraid you'll think less of me when I tell you. So afraid I'll lose this…" She gestured between them. "Your—your friendship… You."

Suddenly it became very important to be there for her. To support her. To communicate the depth of his regard for her.

"It's okay." He draped his arm around her. "Tell me whatever you want. Or not. I'm right here. I'm not going anywhere."

She closed her eyes. "I met Wall Phillips at a party. He was intelligent and handsome. Educated. Well-dressed. A successful businessman. I was flattered someone like him was interested in me."

Luke's gut clenched.

"I didn't see behind the carefully cultivated mask

until it was too late. Until I'd quit my job and moved into his expensive house. That's when I realized, despite the outward trappings, he was no different than my father and brothers." She took a quick, indrawn breath. "He was actually worse. For all his failings, my father never lifted his hand to me."

"How long were you and Wall together?" he forced himself to ask.

"A year." Her eyes flew open. "People always wonder why I didn't just leave. I wanted to. But Wall controlled every aspect of my life. He kept me isolated and totally dependent on him. I was terrified of what he'd do to me if I tried to run."

She went on to tell him about how eventually Wall's white-collar crimes caught up with him. How, when he was sent to jail, she discovered she was pregnant.

"I called him at the prison and told him about the baby. He was explicit about his feelings regarding a child." Her eyes blurred with tears. "That's when I knew I had to run while I had the chance. I couldn't allow Wall to do to my baby what my father had done to my brothers."

Luke's arm tightened around her, holding her close. Her sharing this with him was such a tremendous step. He felt honored she'd trusted him enough to tell him about the hard places in her past. It was a privilege and a responsibility he didn't take lightly.

"Wall wasn't interested in my life before we met. I'm not sure why I ran to Truelove, but I did. Kara gave me a job at the café. When my photo appeared in the paper after the tornado, I got spooked that one of Wall's cronies would recognize me and tell him my whereabouts."

"But he was in prison, right?"

"It was healthier not to ask too many questions about Wall's business associates, but I knew his reach extended far outside the prison."

"Where did you go?"

"Kara put me in touch with a maternity home for women in Durham. She and Trudy were the only ones I told about the baby. The people there were good to me during the last months of my pregnancy. And once I held Jeremiah in my arms the first time?" Tears trickled down her cheeks. "I knew I'd die before I ever let him go."

It gutted him at a physical level to realize all she'd glossed over. The hurt she'd endured at the hands of a monster. How afraid she must have felt giving birth alone to her precious son.

"Then a few weeks ago, I learned that Wall's conviction was overturned on a technicality, and I realized he'd come looking for me."

"What made you decide to come back to True-love?"

She took a shuddering breath. "I'm not sure. I almost didn't. But I read once about sea turtles on the Eastern Shore of Virginia. No matter how far they wander, they always return to the beach where they were born to hatch their eggs. I didn't mean to come this way. All I could think about was getting over the state line. But there was just something about Truelove that drew me. That called me to come and find h-home."

Breaking into sobs, she hung her head.

He tilted her head to look at him. "Don't cry." He brushed away a tear with the pad of his thumb. "You're safe now. I'd never let anyone hurt you or Jeremiah."

She gave him a tremulous smile. "I feel so safe in Truelove. With you. Safer than I've ever felt in my entire life." Her forehead creased. "But you must despise me."

"You're the strongest woman I know," he rasped. "It must have taken such courage to extract yourself from an impossible situation, and you did it twice. Once with your family and then with Wall. And somehow you managed to survive with your humanity intact. I admire you so much for the obstacles you've overcome."

He pressed his forehead against hers. Her lips trembled. And she looked at him with those fathomless blue eyes of hers.

Rising on her toes, she wound her arms around his neck. "Luke." She lifted her face to his. He lowered his head. Only a hair's breadth separated them. Their breath mingled in the frosty air.

Gently he brushed his lips across her cheek. Then his mouth drifted to hers. When he would have pulled away, she cradled his face in the palms of her hands and kissed him back.

There was a rightness in her kiss. An undeniable truth. As inexorable as the tide, or the moon rising over the mountain. Just as she'd said.

It was like coming home.

Shayla hadn't believed it possible to be so happy. *Thank You, Lord. Thank You for this beautiful new beginning.* After last night, she had let go of her fears and doubts. And allowed herself to believe her life might be full of bright possibilities.

Luke's kiss—that glorious, butterflies-dancing-in-her-belly kiss—had expressed his heart for her, even if he wasn't yet ready to say the words out loud.

On Monday morning, she and Mrs. Stewart met over coffee at the Mason Jar to finalize plans for the children's portion of the upcoming Advent service. And in large part because of that amazing kiss last night, Shayla found herself sharing a Christmas lullaby she'd composed. Sight-reading the piece in the booth at the café, Mrs. Stewart hummed the melody line.

Lacing her hands together under the table, her heart pounded as she awaited her mentor's verdict.

Mrs. Stewart glanced up from the paper. Tears shone in her eyes. "The words… Oh, Shayla…"

"I wasn't sure about the second line. I could change—"

"You mustn't change a thing. Not a single thing." Reaching across the table, Mrs. Stewart gripped her hand. "This is so lovely. So perfect for the program. Would you allow us to include it in this year's service?"

She blinked. "You mean you like it?"

"I love it." Mrs. Stewart smiled. "And of course, to do it justice, you must sing it."

"What?" Her eyes grew large. "I—I…"

"Please say you will. Your voice has been a wonderful addition to the choir." Mrs. Stewart patted her hand. "But you are not background vocal material." She waved the paper between them. "You are this, and so much more."

The days that followed were filled to the brim with extra choir rehearsals, sharing the work on the farm and preparing for the holidays. It snowed again. Just enough to keep the temperatures Christmassy, and transforming the town and surrounding mountains into a breathtaking winter wonderland.

Best of all, though, she and Luke, often as not with Jeremiah, spent a lot of time together. The girls were returning from college on Friday. Emily was back on her feet again, yet Dr. Jernigan continued to be a nightly guest for dinner.

"Nothing like making a pest of yourself," Luke griped.

Out in the barn on Thursday evening with him, she prepared to head over to the church for another rehearsal with the children. She was borrowing his truck tonight because of the recent inclement weather.

"Be careful driving," he mentioned, while his cell beeped. "Road might be slick, Shay."

Goose bumps broke out on her skin at the nickname he'd begun to call her. She liked to believe it his own personal term of endearment.

He dug the phone out of his jean pocket and glanced at the screen. "It's Zach again."

Zach was the only pinprick in the bubble of her happiness. Him and getting rid of the only thing that linked her to Wall.

"If I didn't know better, I'd think you were dodging his calls." Luke handed the phone to her. "He needs to talk to you before moving forward on scrapping the vehicle. I think he has an interested buyer for the parts."

Careful not to display her reluctance, she pressed the phone to her ear. "Hello?"

"Shayla?" Zach's voice boomed in her ear. "You're one hard lady to track down. With Christmas coming, I'm under a time crunch here. If it's compensation you're worried about, I promise I'll give you fair market value. I wouldn't cheat you."

Luke turned away to fiddle with something on the workbench.

She rubbed her forehead. "I know you wouldn't, Zach."

"I really need the title on file before I begin dismantling the car. Can I run over to the house tonight and get it from you?"

"Uh…um… There's been an unavoidable delay in getting the title to you. I don't have the title with me in Truelove."

"Oh." His voice went deep. "I didn't realize. A little more complicated but not a disaster. You can apply for a duplicate title online with the DMV. The form will have to be notarized, but Myra Penry, my aunt, can take care of that for you. Just requires your driver's license number, a replacement fee and the VIN number. Vehicle Identification—"

"I know what a VIN number is, Zach."

One of her earliest memories was of her father teaching her older brothers how to file off and deface the number located in various parts of an automobile, prior to fencing.

"No worries, though, Shayla. I can get the VIN number off the car and give you a call tomorrow."

She squeezed her eyelids shut. This was what

she'd feared happening from the beginning. Assuming Wall hadn't filed off the number—which in itself would raise suspicions the automobile was stolen—once Zach ran the number, he'd know for sure she wasn't the owner.

And that she was a car thief. No better than her brothers or her father. And worse, running the number might somehow alert Wall to her location. For Jeremiah's sake, not to mention her own, that must never be allowed to happen.

"But since it's you," Zach droned on. "And I know you'll get the title to me sooner or later, with your permission, I might just go ahead this weekend when I've got some free time to begin stripping the car. The buyer won't wait forever."

If he was in that big of a hurry, perhaps he wouldn't stop to run the VIN number at all.

"Do what you need to do for your client, Zach." She held her breath, waiting for his response.

"Thanks for working through this with me, Shayla." He clicked off.

She stared at the phone. She hated—absolutely hated—deceiving the mechanic. He was a good guy. Always decent to her at the Mason Jar, and back in high school, too.

"Anything wrong?"

Hoping her hand didn't shake, she handed Luke his phone. "What could be wrong?"

Luke's dark eyes warmed. "Nothing, when I look at you."

She fluttered her lashes. "You're getting pretty good with the sweet nothings."

"You inspire me." He pulled her close. She thought he might kiss her again, but after a quick hug he let her go. "Have a good rehearsal."

On the drive to church, she reflected on her conversation with Zach. Situation averted. Problem contained. Or at least she hoped so.

She and Luke hadn't kissed again. But she remained optimistic for a repeat performance of their kiss. Humming under her breath, she pulled into the church parking lot feeling hopeful about so much.

Most of all, that finally she'd managed to outrun her past.

The rehearsal went well. The children were eager to sing. She did her best to make it fun for them. Her goal was for them to associate fun and music with God. And she was surprised how much she enjoyed teaching music to Truelove's youngest citizens.

The last one out of the building, she flicked off the lights and clicked the exterior door shut behind her.

A shadow emerged from the enormous rhododendron beside the path. "Shayla."

Even before she whirled, she knew that voice.

All too well. Her stomach plummeted. She gazed longingly at Luke's truck, parked under a utility light. No sign of another vehicle. He must've parked out of sight down the road.

Her father, Dol Coggins, blocked her escape. "Long time no see, baby girl."

Not long enough. She gripped the car key between her index and middle fingers.

Her father shot a pointed look at her hand. "You planning on using that on me?"

"No, Daddy." She forced herself to breathe. "What do you want?"

He shook his shaggy, graying head. "Why do you assume I've come wanting something, Shayla Rae?"

Because he always did.

"You wound me, girl, when all I've come to do is warn you about a man poking around the holler asking questions about you." Her father whistled. "From the slick looks of him, you've been 'sociating with folks in the high-rent district."

Wall. Her gut roiled. "What did you tell him?"

"Give me some credit," Dol Coggins hissed. "Despite how you've treated your kin, to me blood is thicker than water. I put him off. But he's not the kind to quit looking."

She studied her father. He'd aged since she last saw him. When she learned he was being paroled after his latest incarceration, she'd known if she was ever going to escape her family, she had to do it then.

Yet she'd fled from the frying pan straight into the fire with Wall. Dol had been a handsome man once. But life was catching up to him.

Her father, never the paternal type, scrubbed his face. "If I can locate you, eventually he will, too."

"Thank you for telling me, Daddy."

She should've known the selfless concern, if that indeed was what it was, never lasted long with him. *Wait for it...*

"You better hightail it out of here, girl." His gaze cut to the Morgan Farm logo on Luke's truck. "Before you bring trouble down on the good people who've taken your worthless self into their lives."

And there it was.

Looking away, she didn't bother telling him he had a grandson. He wouldn't have cared. And if he did, it would have only been to use her baby to make a buck. She'd not put her child in Dol Coggins's crosshairs.

When she glanced back, he was gone. Disappearing into the night as quickly as he'd appeared. A master of the quick getaway.

Though she might try with all her might to escape her past, she feared her past might never let go of her.

Chapter Eleven

❧

The next day, on Friday, Luke's sisters returned home for Christmas break. Everyone gathered in the living room. Krista had big news.

"I applied for an internship next year." Her brown eyes flitted between her mom and her brother. "I got it."

Emily hugged her. "That's wonderful, honey."

Shayla clapped. "How exciting."

Caroline tucked a tendril of dark hair behind her ear. "Tell them the rest, Kris."

"The internship is in London."

Luke frowned. "London, England?"

Gulping, she nodded.

Emily's smile faltered, but only for a second. "What an adventure you'll have."

Krista looked at her brother. "Maybe I should stick closer to home so I can help you and Mom with the farm."

He fingered his chin. "Is this something you want to do?"

Krista's mouth wobbled. "I've dreamed of doing it since I first heard about the program."

"Then I think…"

Krista gulped.

Shayla held her breath. She knew how much Krista trusted her brother's judgment. He held the power in his hands to completely crush her hopes or give her the strength to pursue her dreams.

"We'll always be here for you, little sister, but I think you should go."

"Really?"

He hugged her. "I'm so proud of you, Krissy."

Later on, in the kitchen, Shayla pulled him aside. "I'm so proud of you for encouraging Krista to follow her dreams. I know how protective you are of her."

He gave her a small smile. "Here's something I learned from my dad. Other than Jesus, roots and wings are the most important things we can gift those we love."

She tilted her head. "Roots and wings?"

"Each of us needs roots, sunk deep in the soil of home, to enable us to flourish. But at the same time, we need the gift of wings to give us the courage to fly."

A gift of both. Her eyes misted. The matchmakers were right. Kind. Devoted. Self-sacrificing. He really would make the most extraordinary husband and father someday.

She watched him out the window as he headed to the barn. Plus, he was oh-so easy on the eyes. Her heart fluttered.

Midmorning, she borrowed Emily's SUV to drive into town. Miss IdaLee had phoned and asked her to stop by her house. The elderly schoolteacher had a gift for Jeremiah.

She parked at the curb in front of the cheerily decorated Victorian. IdaLee met her at the door. "Come in."

IdaLee ushered her inside. "Charles and I are making peanut butter balls for our family's Christmas Eve gathering."

Shayla bit back a smile at the way IdaLee pronounced Charles's name—a dragged-out, two-syllable drawl. According to Lila, IdaLee and her beloved spent most of their waking hours in each other's company.

Charles poked his head around the door frame of the kitchen and held up sticky hands. "I'd love to chat, but I've made a mess in the kitchen, and I don't want to get on Idaho's naughty list."

She laughed.

The very proper Miss IdaLee rolled her eyes. "Silly man." She gave her love an indulgent smile. "I'll be there directly, Charles."

Waving, he disappeared into the kitchen again.

IdaLee led her into the front parlor to the enormous Morgan Farm Christmas tree. She handed Shayla a small butcher-paper-wrapped package. The schoolteacher was renowned for her gift-giving.

"Thank you so much." Shayla fingered the blue silk ribbon. "For thinking of Jeremiah."

"It's a book." IdaLee patted her arm. "Promise me you'll read to him every night. It's important to build language skills."

Shayla hugged her. "I promise I will. No matter where we find ourselves, I'll read to him every night."

The old woman squinted at her. "You want to leave Truelove?"

Shayla clutched the gift. "I'm struggling to know what I should do to be true to myself."

"To be true to yourself, you have to listen to your heart. What is your heart saying? What is your heart telling you to do?"

Shayla swallowed. "I'm afraid to trust my heart."

The old woman's violet gaze flickered. "Forty years ago, I let my head talk my heart out of what I knew to be right, and I regretted it every day of my life until last Saturday."

From the kitchen, Charles called for IdaLee.

"I should let you go." Shayla took a breath. "I need to get back to Jeremiah."

At the door, IdaLee touched her cheek. "I'll be praying for you, dear heart. That the Lord guides you to the right choice for you and your precious boy."

Leaving the older woman, she made her way to the sidewalk. Unlocking the SUV, the hairs on her neck tingled. She had the strangest sensation she was being watched. Looking around, she didn't spot anything out of the ordinary.

Probably a by-product of Wall-induced paranoia. She shook off the weird, unsettling vibe and got in the car. She resolved to put her no-good exboyfriend out of her mind for good.

Christmas was in a week. Jeremiah's first. A first with Luke's family. Would it also be their last? Oh, how she hoped not.

She prayed all the way to the farm for God to make a place in Truelove for her and her baby.

When she reached the house, she was surprised to see Luke sitting alone on the porch steps, his phone in his hand. She would have driven into the garage, but he rose and came over. He looked exhausted.

She stopped and scrolled the window down. "Everything all right? How come you're sitting out here alone in the cold?"

He stuffed the cell into his pocket. "I got the call from the bank."

She switched off the engine and hopped out of the car. "I'm so happy for—"

"It wasn't good news, Shay." He took a breath. "Or at least not the news we expected. The bank denied my application for the loan extension."

"Oh, Luke." She threw her arms around him. "I'm so sorry."

He held her for a long, long moment.

"Your mom and the girls must be so upset."

"I haven't told them yet." His arms tightened around her. "I found myself wanting to tell you. I just needed to talk with you first."

He'd needed her. He'd wanted to confide in her. Something welled in her heart. He clung to her for another minute.

"You worked so hard to make this happen," she whispered against his ear.

"I feel dazed. I feel disappointment, but not despair." He pulled away slightly, but he didn't let her drift far from the circle of his arms. "I can't explain it. Other than to say, despite everything, I feel this incredible sense of peace."

She tilted her head.

"I've been praying for God to make a way for the farm to continue, but the answer is no." Luke leaned his forehead against hers. "More than a small part of me is relieved. We lost seven seasons of trees due to the blight. And those in-between years when we had to regrow our entire stock placed us in tremendous debt. We were never able to catch up. The loan wouldn't have solved that. Only put us deeper into a hole we couldn't climb out of."

She hugged him tight, willing her strength and comfort to him.

He sighed. "Instead of giving in to despair, I've decided to follow your example. To put into practice what I've learned from you."

She let go of him. "From me?"

"You taught me to trust God. No matter what. God may have shut out the opportunity with the bank." He cradled her face in his palms. "But that just means He has a better plan. I'm going to trust Him to show me His best for me."

She gazed deep into his eyes. "Have I told you, Luke Morgan, how proud I am of the man you've become?"

Luke gave her the sweetest smile. "Have I told you, Shayla Coggins, how lovely you are—inside and out?"

He lowered his head. Rising on the toes of her boots, she lifted her face. His kiss was tender. Gentler than the first kiss they shared. But it still left her breathless.

Luke ran his finger across the apple of her cheek. "There will be a bank auction at the end of January. I wanted to have you by my side when

I broke the news to Mom and the girls. They'll be devastated."

She gripped his arm. "You did everything you could."

He blew out a breath. "Whatever the future holds for me and Morgan Tree Farm, I trust God to do the rest."

They went in together to talk to his family. And she knew right then there was no place she'd rather be than at his side.

Luke's family took the news surprisingly well.

His gaze roamed from his mother to Caroline to Krista. "I can't tell you how sorry I am for losing our home."

"You haven't lost us our home." His mom drew him into an embrace. "This farm doesn't define us or home. Our true home is with the Lord."

"My greatest regret is letting everyone down."

Krista wrapped her arms around his middle. "You haven't let us down. You've been the best big bro ever."

"And the best son." His mom touched his face. "Your father would be so proud of how you've held the farm and this family together."

Luke hunched his shoulders. "Would he, Mom?"

"Yes, he would." She lifted her chin. "God is doing a new thing for the Morgans."

Seated on the couch beside Shayla, Caroline

had remained uncharacteristically silent. "Are you okay, Caro?"

"I am." She got off the sofa. "But you look like you could use cheering up. I have an early Christmas present for you."

She rooted under the Christmas tree and brought out a large gift bag. "Merry Christmas, Luke. I love you."

"I love you, too, but what's this?" He glanced at his mom, who simply smiled. "We don't unwrap gifts until Christmas morning."

"Go ahead." Krista bounced over to his recliner and perched on the edge. "I can't wait for you to see what Caroline got you for Christmas this year."

He pulled out the tissue paper to find a glossy copy of the regional Southern lifestyle magazine. "I don't understand."

Caroline fluttered her hand. "Flip it open."

In the center of the magazine, he found a print-out of typed pages. "Okayyy…"

She gave a dramatic sigh. "For the love of Christmas trees, Luke, read the title and the by-line."

He studied the top of the page. "'*The Moonlight Tree*. By Luke Morgan.'" His head snapped up. "This is the story I wrote about the tree on the ridge."

"A special tree planted by his grandfather." His mom looked at Shayla. "No matter how hard the times, the tree no Morgan ever cuts. We used to decorate it with treats for the animals every year."

"Our Christmas gift to the other creatures that live in these mountains with us." Caroline's gaze never wandered from his. "But after Dad died, we stopped. It was like the heart of the farm went with him."

Luke scanned the pages. "One Christmas Eve when we were young, Dad took us out in the snow at midnight to see the tree."

"Because I wanted to see the animals." Krista smiled. "It was a full moon that night, shining down on the snow."

Caroline nodded. "A special memory. I've never forgotten it. You captured every perfect detail in your story."

"But I still don't—"

"We were wrong about the heart going out of this farm. *You* are the heart of this farm, Luke." His sister clasped her hands together. "It's a beautiful story. A story that needed to be told. That others beyond our family needed to read."

His breath hitched. "What did you do?"

"I printed out copies of the stories you keep in the folder on your laptop."

He recalled several occasions over the summer and as recently as Thanksgiving when he'd found his computer open and Caroline in his office.

"I showed them to my English professor."

Wincing, he rubbed his forehead. "They were drafts. They needed a lot of polishing."

"He didn't think they needed much tinkering. Neither did the journalist who wrote the *Christmas in Carolina* edition. AnnaBeth's mom put me in touch with him."

Luke vaguely recalled Caroline in deep conversation with Victoria Cummings during Open House weekend.

"And the magazine editor agreed. She said your story captured the essence of the Blue Ridge, family and home." Caroline looked at him. "They want to publish the story in next year's *Christmas in Carolina* edition."

"My story?" He blinked at her. "They want my story?"

Caroline smiled. "Not only the one, but several others in the folder, too. After Christmas, the editor wants to meet with you. To discuss future writing projects. You're a writer, Luke. This is what you were made for."

Shayla's hand went to her throat. "Oh, Caroline. This is wonderful."

"I can't believe this is happening." Stunned, he could only stare at her. "You did this? For me? Why?"

Caroline's mouth trembled. "Because you sacrificed so much for Mom, Krista and me. It was past time for your dreams to come true."

"Thank you, Caroline. This is the best Christmas gift ever."

He pulled his no-longer-pesky sister into a hug. Which soon became a hug fest as each of the Morgans rose to express their joy for him. Krista pulled Shayla in, as well.

Theirs was such a demonstrative family. And he wouldn't trade any of them for the world, much less a byline.

Thank You, God. For the chance to pursue my writing dream. And for my family.

Luke's gaze flew to Shayla. "Did you know about this?"

Her eyes glistened. "No, but it couldn't have happened to a more deserving person. Congratulations, Luke."

There was the sound of tires crunching gravel from the driveway. Krista floated to the window. "Do you know why Miss IdaLee and her boyfriend are here?"

Luke headed toward the door. "I forgot Mr. Redfern texted me yesterday."

"Wait." Krista's brow creased. "An old guy like him texts?"

Caroline groaned. The rest of them laughed.

"Anyway…" Luke chuckled. "He said he was interested in seeing our operation, and wanted a private tour." He shrugged. "I figured, why not?"

But the hour he'd anticipated giving Charles and

IdaLee turned into three. And included a conversation he never in his wildest dreams could have imagined.

More than a little gobsmacked, he stood in front of the house waving as Charles and IdaLee drove away late that afternoon.

"Hey." Shayla came out to stand beside him. "We were getting worried. Is everything all right?"

"Better than all right." Grabbing her waist, he lifted her off her feet and whirled her around. "Fantastic. Marvelous. Amazing."

"Put me down, Luke." Laughing, she wound her arms around his shoulders. "What's got you so excited now?"

He set her on her feet. "Mr. Redfern wanted to see every square inch of the farm. Every row of trees." He grinned. "This is the best day ever."

She hugged his arm. "I'm so happy about your byline."

"Not only that. Turns out after Mr. Redfern and Miss IdaLee split up all those years ago, he left the military. And I'm delighted to tell you he bought a small, struggling grocery store in Florida."

She narrowed her eyes. "Are you sure you're feeling okay?" She touched the back of her hand to his forehead. "It's not like you to get worked up over retail."

"His grocery store is no longer small or struggling." He broadened his shoulders. "Ever heard of Farm to Fork?"

"Sure, it's a specialty gourmet chain with stores all over the United States." She gasped. "Miss Ida-Lee's beau owns that?"

"They source their products from small farmers. His lawyers are emailing the contract on Monday, but Shayla…" Luke gulped. "Charles Redfern bought the next seven harvests of Christmas trees."

Her mouth dropped.

"Mr. Redfern is a national distributor. Morgan Christmas trees will be available everywhere."

"Exactly what you said you needed to make Morgan Farm viable." Her lips trembled. "God is so good."

Yes, He is. Sunshine or rain. Blight or bumper crop.

He released a breath. "God closed the door to more debt with the bank."

She kissed his cheek. "And opened this better opportunity instead."

Unaccustomed moisture blurred his vision. *Thank You, God. For allowing us to keep this patch of land we've always called home. Thank You.*

"Now you can grow Christmas trees. And write about them, too." She hung on his arm. "Roots and wings. You were right. This is the best day ever."

* * *

Saturday was busy. It was the last choose-and-cut weekend of the season. But his heart was light. There would be more seasons, more years to enjoy the land God had seen fit to allow him to steward.

And he was in awe of the possibilities God was working in their lives. Caroline's boyfriend came to dinner on Saturday. Luke had to grudgingly admit the guy wasn't half-bad.

But he hardly saw Shayla over the next twenty-four hours. She was in a whirlwind of final rehearsals for the upcoming family service taking place Sunday night.

Her old friend from the Mason Jar, Trudy, talked Shayla into allowing her to babysit Jeremiah at the farmhouse so the entire Morgan clan could cheer her on at the church.

There was to be the usual hot cocoa and cookies in the fellowship hall afterward. That evening, his mom, Caroline and Krista left early with their baking contributions to help set up the tables. Leaving him to escort Shayla to church for the choir's call time. Trudy took Jeremiah into the kitchen for his supper.

Luke waited for Shayla at the door. When she came down the stairs, she took his breath away. Her blond hair lay loose across her shoulders. Set against the silky red blouse she wore, her skin glowed.

She smoothed her hand across her black skirt. "Do I look okay?"

He swallowed, hard. "You look…you look beautiful."

She took a deep breath. "Please pray I don't mess up the solo."

He took her hand. "You won't mess up. This is your time to shine. To show Truelove they better sit up and take notice of the supertalented Shayla Coggins."

"Not sure that last part is true." She gave him a small smile. "But thank you. You make me believe I can do anything."

Funny, because that's how she made him feel, too.

Perhaps Friday hadn't been his best day, after all. Because when he looked at her, he reckoned his best day ever might have been the day her car broke down on the mountain.

Gratitude filled his heart for how God had brought Shayla and Jeremiah into his life.

Chapter Twelve

On Sunday evening, the church was so lovely it took Shayla's breath away. Sitting in the choir loft, she fought a battle with her nerves. A chair creaked. Pages rustled.

She clutched the black music folder to her chest. She and her fellow choir members waited for the lights to dim and the program to begin.

The sanctuary continued to fill for the much-anticipated Advent service. It appeared everyone in Truelove had decided to attend. Her stomach knotted.

It had been a long time since she'd sung a solo. Since high school. It was one thing to sing to Jeremiah, but there were so many people here…

She scanned the congregation. Kara and Will. AnnaBeth and Jonas. Lila, her parents, Sam and an older, scholarly looking man she didn't recognize. The McAbees. Police Chief Hollingsworth and Maggie.

She flicked a glance to where Luke sat with his family. Caroline and Krista. Emily and Dr. Jernigan. Third row from the front. They'd catch every missed note.

Why had she thought she could do this?

She ran her hand along the buttery smoothness of the crushed velvet black skirt. Used to jeans and secondhand clothing from thrift stores, she'd never felt so elegant in her life. Kara and Caroline had taken her to the outlet mall on the highway to outfit her for the service. Despite her protests, the Mason Jar chef had declared it a Christmas gift for her big night.

Big night? Some big night. Right now, it was all she could do to resist the urge to bolt out of her chair and run.

If only the music would start. She'd be fine once the music began to play.

No surprise the matchmakers had claimed an entire pew for themselves. Seated beside Bill, ErmaJean waved. Next to her not-so-secret boyfriend, Walter, GeorgeAnne arched her brow. But with a single, tiny nod, it was IdaLee, alongside her beloved Charles, who gave her the affirmation she sorely needed.

A reminder that the people of Truelove—and most especially those here tonight—were her friends. They believed in her. They believed in her talent.

This was her town. Her community. An acknowledgment of acceptance. The belonging she'd been searching for her entire life.

All her friends were here to support her with their presence and faith in her.

So instead of continuing to unravel with self-doubt, she concentrated on imprinting the details of this evening on her memory forever. She took a quick breath.

The tangy aroma of evergreen boughs perfumed the air inside the sanctuary. In the window casement lining the walls, white pillar candles flickered from within lantern globes.

Swags of garland bedecked the choir loft. Morgan Farm greenery. Her gaze drifted to Luke. He gave her a small thumbs-up and smiled.

Mrs. Stewart took her place at the lectern on the platform. It was time. Shayla's heart did a quick, staccato beat.

Baton in hand, Mrs. Stewart raised her arms. The house lights dimmed. At her cue, Shayla and the choir rose as one. Her breath hitched. Mrs. Stewart signaled the pianist. The music began.

Shayla opened her mouth to sing. And as the notes poured forth from her throat, her fears were forgotten in the glory of once again making music.

"Come, all ye faithful. Joyful and triumphant. Come ye, O come ye to Bethlehem."

Her eyes flitted toward the Nativity crèche on the altar. This was what she'd been made for. Her voice. Her life.

A small but heartfelt offering to the Christ Child.

Although Shayla claimed there was a sort of lyricism to the words in the stories he penned about his home in the Blue Ridge, Luke wasn't musical. Never had been.

The choir led the congregational singing. When it came time for their song in the program, the children were adorable as they took their places on the steps at the altar rail.

Shayla slipped from her place in the loft and crouched in front of her small charges. He snuck a look at his youngest sister as she edged out of the pew and joined Shayla. Krista had enjoyed helping with the pint-size choir. All the little girls wore white tights, black patent leather shoes and fancy dresses with matching red headbands. The little boys sported matching red bow ties.

Sitting on her heels, Krista touched the corners of her mouth to remind the children to smile. Little Emma Cate fluttered her fingers at her dad. Luke grinned at Sam, who beamed as only a proud papa could. His adopted daughter hung the moon in his eyes. Which was entirely the way it should be.

The way Luke felt about baby Jeremiah.

He scanned the faces of the other men around him. Some of the children were their flesh and blood. Like Jake McAbee, Jonas Stone and Will MacKenzie. But many were not. As with Ethan Green and Bridger Hollingsworth.

Yet each one had become the child of their heart. Which, in the end, was all that mattered.

He yearned to be counted as worthy as them, to be the sort of father Jeremiah deserved.

Shayla caught the children's attention, and they straightened and focused. She gave a nod to the pianist. The lively, upbeat song was about a donkey, a sheep and a camel at the manger in a Bethlehem stable.

All the moms, dads and grandparents got out their phones to record the performance. Kara sat on the edge of the pew, lip-synching every word along with her new son, Maddox, undeniably cute in his crisp, long-sleeved white cotton shirt and bow tie.

The vocal trio part became more of a musical comedy duet when the exuberant Green twins jockeyed for best position at the mic. Cheeks pink, Amber just shook her head. Tears of mirth leaked from Ethan's eyes.

With a wisdom beyond his years, young lasso champion Hunter Stone took a giant sidestep out of the fray and let the girls carry on without him. His raised eyebrows said it all.

Hilarious. So Truelove. Exactly what the Christmas family service should be. The song concluded, and Shayla rose to her feet, leading the applause. The children beamed, pride in their accomplishment evident on their faces.

The children filed off the steps. Shayla went out of her way to make sure that, with a touch, look or word, each child knew they had done a great job. Krista led the children back to their doting parents. Shayla returned to the choir loft.

Reverend Bryant took his place beside the glowing lights of the Advent wreath. "Now, that's going to be a hard act to follow." He grinned. "But I'll do my best."

Everyone laughed.

He opened his Bible and read from selected passages. There were other choir numbers, reflecting on the sacredness of the season, but as the time drew nearer for Shayla's solo, Luke returned to being a nervous wreck.

His palms went sweaty. He felt as jumpy as a Christmas tree in the baler. Krista laid her hand on top of his jiggly knee.

"Stop it," she hissed.

"Calm down." Caroline glared at him. "Shayla's got this. Have a little faith, why don't you?"

He wanted her to succeed so badly. Especially

here in her hometown, where she'd struggled her entire life to find a place for herself.

Pangs of anxiety were doing somersaults inside his chest on her behalf. And if he was feeling it, what must she be feeling?

He had no doubt that eventually she would sing on countless stages to wide acclaim.

But perhaps here in Truelove tonight mattered more than anywhere else.

Then it was time for the final song of the evening. She came out from the loft and stood at the edge of the platform. The lights dimmed once more. The spotlight shone on her lovely face.

He could tell she was nervous only because he knew her so well. There was a slight tightening of her lips. Her eyes narrowed. Mrs. Stewart cued the young man on the fiddle. But when Shayla began to sing, all traces of tension vanished.

There was only the music. The words she'd painstakingly penned. The emotion in the inflection of her voice.

And he stopped worrying for her. This was who she was. This was what she'd been made for.

He'd happened to hear snatches of the song as she went about caring for Jeremiah, caring for his mother, caring for him. But this was the first time he'd heard the song from beginning to end with instrumental accompaniment. Her lovely contralto voice began soft, gentle and low.

The song was a cradle lullaby, a mother's love for her child. A love for her Savior born this night. The melody had a melancholy, bittersweet undertone that hinted of a cross yet to be borne. It reminded Luke of the Appalachian ballads the old-timers in Truelove used to sing.

Its beauty was in its simplicity. A deceptive simplicity that built in intensity until the climax. Her face glowed with the passion of the words. But when the perspective of the song returned to the cradle, peaceful and serene, she closed her eyes.

The last exquisite note hung in the air, floating to the rafters. There was a hushed stillness. The audience savored the sheer beauty of the performance, sensing what they'd just witnessed was nothing short of extraordinary. A once-in-a-lifetime experience. As if everyone was as reluctant as him to let the moment go.

And then the applause began. Thunderous. Her eyes snapped open. The congregation rose in a standing ovation. There were smiles. More than a few tears streamed down faces. His mother and sisters openly wept.

Taken aback, Shayla's gaze darted to her teacher. Her face aglow, Mrs. Stewart tucked the baton under her arm and clapped. The choir, too, joined in the applause. Shayla put a hand to her throat.

Her lips parting, surprise wrinkled the smooth

lines of her forehead. And he realized that during her song she'd forgotten anyone else was there. She'd been singing to an audience of One.

Thank You, Lord. Thank You for giving her this night. This song. This gift.

He wiped the moisture from his eyes. The song had been incredible. She had been radiant.

Shaking like a beech leaf in a winter's gale, she slipped back into the loft. Mrs. Stewart invited the congregation to join the choir in a final carol, "Joy to the World." Young and old, men, women, teenagers and children sang their heartfelt praise to the Savior.

Swiping her fingers under the rims of her glasses, GeorgeAnne threaded her arm through Walter's. IdaLee's reedy voice grew stronger with each note. ErmaJean made a joyful noise.

Reverend Bryant said a benediction. People dispersed, headed toward the fellowship hall for cookies and cocoa. Luke followed the musicians returning their music folders to the choir room.

Outside in the hallway, he leaned against the wall and waited for Shayla. IdaLee and Charles found him there.

"How's the writing going?"

"Great." Straightening, he shook Charles's hand. "This was the last choose-and-cut weekend at the farm. The tree lot closes tomorrow. I've been jotting down ideas. I'm looking forward to having more time to flesh them out into stories."

"You and Shayla have made quite a team this Christmas tree season." IdaLee smiled. "Though it's no surprise to me. Creative hearts are drawn to other creative hearts. Sparking off each other. Inspiring each other to further creativity."

Shayla came out of the choir room. His pulse quickened. She blushed when their gazes locked.

IdaLee gave Charles a fond glance. "Let's give Truelove's little songbird and future literary laureate some breathing room." The older couple shuffled off toward the fellowship hall.

"Was it okay?" She pressed his arm. "Could you understand every word? Was every note clear?"

"Better than okay." He squeezed her hand. "You were magnificent."

She gave her head a tiny shake as if she didn't believe him. "That's kind of you to say."

"I'm not being kind. I'm telling you the truth."

As soon as they strolled into the fellowship hall, she didn't have to take only his word for it. She was immediately surrounded by others echoing his praise.

"I'll be over here." He let go of her hand. "To give your new fans better access."

Her forehead creased. "Luke…"

"You'll be fine." He winked. "Can I get you

something to drink?" He gestured at the refreshment table.

"Thank you. Maybe some iced tea?"

No sooner had he stepped aside than she was swallowed by Truelove well-wishers. Over the matchmakers' trio of graying heads, she threw him a slightly desperate glance.

He chuckled as he made his way to the food. When he returned, a small line had formed, waiting for the chance to congratulate her. He handed her a cup of sweet tea.

She took a long swallow. Finally, she came up for air. "Thanks."

"No problem. Can I snag you a cookie or something?"

He would have moved away, but she caught his arm, anchoring him close by her side. "Don't leave me," she whispered.

"Wouldn't dream of it." He nudged her gently. "But you better get used to your adoring fans."

She wrinkled her nose at him. "As long as you stay right here and count yourself among them."

He leaned closer, his mouth brushing the strands of hair at her ear. "Shay, don't you know I'm your number one fan?"

Shayla's cheeks turned a petal-pink shade, and her eyes sparkled. "I may hold you to that, mister."

He laughed, the sound rumbling in his chest. "I'm counting on it."

Lila and a fiftysomething couple were the final ones waiting for a chance to speak with Shayla. With his iron-gray beard and tweed blazer with the elbow patches, the older man looked like a professor. A peppermint-striped scarf dangled from around his neck. The older woman hung on to his arm, and Luke presumed her to be his wife.

"I want you to meet some special friends of mine, Shayla." Lila drew the man forward. "Oliver and Miranda West. Oliver is a visiting lecturer at nearby Ashmont College. In the music department, actually."

Shayla offered her hand. "Hi, I'm—"

"Lila has told me so much about you." The man engulfed Shayla's small hand in his. "Thank you, young lady. For an absolutely incredible, never-to-be-forgotten performance."

Miranda clapped her hands together. "Absolutely stunning."

Shayla cut her eyes at Luke and then Lila. "I'm glad you enjoyed the service. It was a team effort." She eased her hand out of the professor's enthusiastic grasp.

"Oliver is also a music producer." Lila looked at Shayla. "From Nashville. I told him there was someone he had to hear before he headed home for the holidays."

"Me?"

"Of course you." Lila patted her arm. "Oliver

has worked with a number of recording artists through the years."

She mentioned a few well-known country and gospel music performers even Luke had heard of.

"My specialty is contemporary country, but I've always had an intense interest in Southern Appalachian music. I was impressed with your performance." Mr. West shook his head. "I've never heard that song before. Is it an original composition?"

Luke placed his hand in the small of her back. "Shayla wrote the music and words. As you can see from the response tonight, everyone in Truelove is very proud of her. Including me."

She smiled at him.

"Musical composition is a separate gift than performance." Oliver West fingered his beard. "Not everyone can do both. You are extremely talented, Shayla."

Her mouth wobbled. "Thank you, Mr. West. That means so much coming from an expert like you."

"Call me Oliver, please." He smiled. "Lila tells me you're headed to Nashville after the New Year."

Luke's gut tightened at the reminder.

She nodded. "With my son."

His heart twisted.

The music producer tilted his head. "I believe

you could have a bright future ahead of you in either songwriting or performing. Perhaps both."

"You truly think so, Mr.—Oliver?"

"I do. But at the beginning, Nashville can be a tough place to get established on your own." The older man reached into pocket and withdrew a business card. "I'd like to do anything I can to smooth the transition for you."

A sinking feeling roiled in Luke's stomach.

Miranda West shot a fond glance at her husband. "Oliver and I were never able to have children of our own. However, the Lord has blessed us in so many other ways. And over the years, we've enjoyed taking a few young artists under our wing. To advise and nurture them."

Oliver handed Shayla his business card. "I'd like to introduce you to good people who can further your career. Make sure you get off on the right foot."

"God is so good." Tears sprang to her eyes. "Oh, Oliver. Miranda. How can I ever thank you?"

Miranda fluttered her hand. "By using the gifts God gave you to make beautiful music."

"We're making an early start to Tennessee tomorrow morning." Oliver took his wife's hand. "But please contact us when you arrive in Nashville."

"I will." Shayla hugged Lila. "And thank you for bringing the Wests to meet me."

Oliver turned toward the door. "We'll look forward to hearing from you."

His wife smiled. "And I can't wait to meet that beautiful son Lila has told me so much about."

Lila and the Wests headed out of the fellowship hall.

"Did that really just happen?" Shayla grabbed Luke's arm. "A music producer wants to work with me. Or did I imagine it all?"

Torn by conflicting emotions, his temple throbbed. "You didn't imagine it."

"I can't wait to tell your mom." She laughed, the sound as light and airy as Christmas bells. "Where are your sisters?" Bubbling with excitement and energy, she spun around before spotting them. "I'll be back." She touched his arm before dashing away to share her life-changing good news.

He actually wished he *had* imagined what'd just happened. How despicable and selfish was that? Because he wanted to be the one to make Shayla's dreams come true.

Ridiculous, of course. He could never do for her professionally what this Oliver music producer person could. And even more than he dreaded Shayla and Jeremiah no longer being in his life, he wanted the best for Shayla. She deserved the best life had to offer.

There could be no doubt the Lord had orchestrated this turn of events for her. But, try as he might, he couldn't shake a sense of impending personal doom. He would never stand in her way of achieving everything the Lord had in store for her.

He only wished that somehow he, Luke Morgan, could be part of her best life.

Chapter Thirteen

Shayla didn't think she would ever forget last night's Advent service. Everyone had been so encouraging. So supportive. For the first time in her life, she'd felt loved, accepted and cared for.

On Monday morning as the truck clattered over the bridge into Truelove, her gaze flitted to Luke. The tree lot would close for the season at noon. He'd been getting ready to head into town to man the lot for the final time when he'd gotten a text from Zach. With the girls eager to be on Jeremiah duty, she'd volunteered to come along and open up while he went over to the auto shop.

Hands gripping the wheel, Luke circled the square. They drove by places that had become as familiar and as dear to her as its residents. From the number of cars parked outside the restaurant, the Mason Jar was doing a thriving business with the breakfast crowd this morning.

For a single mom, time alone was hard to come by. When Luke went to talk with Zach, she needed to gather her thoughts. About Mr. West and her career. About Truelove. About what she wanted for herself and her son. Most of all, about the man beside her.

Luke pulled in behind the camper.

She knew God had had a purpose in her car breaking down so close to Truelove. And the chance encounter with Luke was part of God's plan for her and Jeremiah's life. A plan for a future.

Luke switched off the engine. "I won't be long."

She stepped out of the truck. "Take your time. You and Zach should get a chocolate croissant at the Jar. I know how you love pastry." She grinned at him.

"Yeah. Well…" Not returning her smile, he threw himself out of the cab. "We'll see."

She hadn't seen him smile since last night at church. "What's wrong?"

He turned toward the square, increasing her sense of unease. "Nothing."

"Luke—"

But shoulders stiff, head bent, he was already walking away. He trudged past the gazebo and then across the green to Zach's shop at the other end. She bit her lip.

Luke had seemed genuinely happy for her when

she joined him after the service. When had that changed? And why?

Her breath fogging in the crisp December morn, she scurried around switching on the string of perimeter lights. With Christmas Eve only a few days away, the remaining selection of trees was sparse.

She crouched to plug the giant inflatable snowman into the power cord. Hands on her knees, she stared at the snowman slowly filling with air.

What did she want for herself and Jeremiah? The prospect of Nashville and a music career no longer beckoned as brightly as it had when she'd been heading west three weeks ago. More and more, Truelove felt like her truest home. The home she'd always yearned for. Not only for herself but her infant son, too.

She'd found a community of faith in the small mountain town. Friends who cared about her. A family of sorts for Jeremiah. But most of all, she'd once again found her teenage hero, Luke. And love.

Love? She sighed. What was the use denying it? No matter whether he ever loved her or not, she loved Luke with an intensity that took her breath away, with a purity of feeling she'd never dared dream could belong to her.

Despite his inexplicable lack of enthusiasm this morning, there was something special between them. Didn't she owe it to herself, her son and Luke to find out if what she felt was something that would last for a lifetime?

A shadow loomed over her. Her gaze darted upward. Before she could scream, he dragged her upright and shoved her against the aluminum siding of the camper.

Wall Phillips leered at her. "Did you think I wouldn't find you? I don't let go so easily of what belongs to me."

She struggled to get free of his grip. "You're hurting me."

"You hurt me by running off with what's mine." He ran the index finger of his other hand the length of her cheek. "Or have you so quickly forgotten what happens to people who disappoint me?"

Wall enjoyed hurting people. She had to be careful not to provoke him.

"I want what you stole from me, Shayla."

"I—"

"Don't lie to me," he muttered. "I've been watching you."

Her blood ran cold, recalling several times over the last few days she'd had the uncanny sensation of being watched.

"I don't know where you've got it stashed, but I want it back." He placed both hands on either side of her head. She shrank back farther. "Cozy little con you've got going on here." He smirked. "Not that I blame you. We were always more alike than we were different."

She stiffened. "I'm nothing like you."

"You're an opportunist. Like your kin. Like me." He shrugged. "Don't get your tail feathers in a twist. I said I didn't blame you." He cut his eyes over his shoulder at the sleepy, unoccupied square. "A new life with the tree farmer. A picture-postcard little town. It's yours for the taking." His eyes slid to hers. "Long as I get what rightfully belongs to me."

Her heart pounded as real fear threatened to overwhelm her. "Jeremiah doesn't belong to you. I won't let you take him."

Wall's head reared a fraction. "Who—oh, the kid." He rolled his eyes. "I told you when you told me you were pregnant, I didn't care what you did with him. I'm talking about my hard-earned cash, Shayla."

Cash? She blinked at him. "I don't—"

"Don't try to double-cross me." He jabbed his finger into her chest. She flinched. "Or maybe I will snatch the kid. As insurance until I get my money back." He got in her face. "Sure would be a shame for that rug rat of yours to go missing."

She cried out. "No!"

"I know where you're staying. Don't try to cheat me. Or you won't be the only one who suffers." His cold blue eyes, as flat and dead as a shark's, scanned the square. "The gazebo. Midnight. Come alone with my money." He sneered. "Or my next visit won't be so cordial."

Then he was gone.

Choking back a sob, she slid down the wall to the ground. What was she going to do? She had no idea what he was talking about. What money? Where was it, and why did he think she could get her hands on it?

She stuffed her fist in her mouth. Despite his clean-cut, investment broker image, she'd learned too late that beneath the pretty boy face and nice manners, Wall Phillips was as mean as a junkyard dog when crossed.

If she couldn't deliver his money, what then? It made her sick to think how she'd placed her son and the entire Morgan family in the crosshairs of a sociopath.

Perhaps she could convince Luke she needed to return to the farmhouse immediately. Grab Jeremiah before Wall could get his dirty hands on him. Persuade one of the girls to drive her to the bus station. She had to get away. She had to go now. She had to protect her son no matter what.

But what about Emily, Caroline and Krista? And Luke... *Oh, dearest God, what should I do about Luke?* Her heart ached with a fierceness she hadn't believed possible.

They'd feel so betrayed. So lied to. And with

her out of his clutches, Wall would only take out his vengeance on them.

She clenched her eyelids shut. *Oh, God, please help me. I'm so scared. What am I going to do?*

With his hands stuffed into his coat pockets, Luke tromped down the sidewalk in front of the elementary school. With students on winter break, the playground was deserted. An empty swing listed to and fro from the wind off the mountain.

His thoughts bleak at the prospect of Shayla leaving town, he shuddered into his coat. Not feeling up to joshing around with the guys on duty, he skirted the fire station.

Luke had lain awake for hours after returning to the farmhouse last night. Contemplating his future—and the lack thereof—without Shayla and Jeremiah. Zach's incoming, beeping text had gotten him out of bed at the crack of dawn: Need to talk ASAP about Shayla's car. Don't say anything to her.

Weird. Slightly troubling. Out of left field. But that was Zach. What was there left to talk about with that rusted heap of junk? Surely he didn't want to renegotiate the payment he'd given Shayla in anticipation of scrapping the vehicle for parts?

She was practically giving him the car for free. Even with her new musical godfather, Oliver West, Shayla and Jeremiah needed the cash. He bunched his shoulders. Zach might be his oldest buddy and friend, but he wasn't going to allow him to railroad her out of rightful compensation.

He jutted his chin. She'd be gone forever soon, but while she was still in Truelove he'd do his dead level best to look out for her interests.

Striding toward the shop, he yanked open the glass-fronted door with a clash of bells. Zach appeared from the office behind the counter.

"Why so mysterious?" Luke grunted. "What's this about Shayla's car?"

Zach wiped his hands on a greasy red cloth. "I thought I ought to talk to you before I called the cops."

His eyes went wide. "What're you talking about? What's her father done now?" His gaze did a quick survey. "Have you been robbed?"

"I haven't been robbed. As far as I know, this has nothing to do with her father." Zach's Adam's apple bobbed. "I meant call the cops on Shayla."

Hackles rising, he took a step forward. "You better watch what you say, Zach Stone." He shook his finger. "And be glad you're standing on the other side of the counter, or I'd—"

"You need to see what I found last night when I took the seats out of the vehicle." Zach's bony face pinched. "She's my friend, too, but I run a legitimate business, Luke."

Not in the best of moods already from too little

sleep and a too early start, he scrubbed his hand over his face. "Show me, then."

Zach gestured toward the open door leading to the garage bay.

Luke charged through into the bay. Zach had been busy dismantling the car since the last time he was here. The raised sedan rested above his head on the car lift. The tires had already been removed. The hood and trunk lids rested against the wall. Much of the vehicle's mechanical guts, the engine parts, lined the workbench.

"The front seat's over there."

Luke skirted around the dilapidated sedan.

Zach rested his palm on top of the seat's uphol-stery. "If I hadn't accidentally snagged the leather, I'd never have noticed the fake backing. But when it came away, I found this."

A cavity had been carved into the cushion on the back of the passenger's seat. Stuffed into the hollow were plastic-wrapped bundles of cash.

Luke inhaled sharply.

Zach lifted his cap, ran his hand over the top of his head and set the ball cap down again. "I can only assume there's probably more stashed on the driver's side, too." He grimaced. "Maybe several other places of concealment I haven't yet found. Drug money."

He stiffened. "We don't know that."

"Dirty money, however it was acquired." Zach

crossed his arms over his blue overalls. "People don't hide legitimate money in the padding of a vehicle."

"Shayla doesn't know about this."

Zach sighed. "You're sure about that, are you? Her family—"

"She's not like them."

"The Cogginses have always kept to themselves for good reason. Or—" Zach made a face "—in their case, no good reason. What do we really know about her, Luke? She shows up out of the blue with a kid—"

"His name is Jeremiah." Luke balled his fist.

"Nobody knew she was pregnant before she left Truelove last spring with no explanation. And now she returns with what's got to be thousands of dollars in cash tucked away in her car. We're not wrong to be suspicious. I'm just saying—"

"And I'm just saying there's no way Shayla is responsible for this." Luke glared at him. "She hates the things her family has done. She ran away to get away from them."

"You're not thinking straight. The facts are the facts."

Luke drew up. "The only fact we know is you found money in her car."

"A lot of money."

"Which could have been put there by anyone." Luke planted his hands on his hips. "Before you go making accusations, consider how she practically gave you the car to scrap. Not something a guilty person would've done if they were hiding stolen money."

Zach mirrored his stance. "Creating this hidey-hole took time. You can't seriously believe she didn't know what somebody was doing to her vehicle."

"She deserves the benefit of the doubt until we can prove otherwise." He lifted his chin. "I don't believe she did this."

Zach snorted. "You don't believe she did this because you don't *want* to believe it. Because you're in love with her."

"I'm not—" His heart hammered. But it was true. "Okay," he whispered. "I am in love with her."

Zach touched his shoulder. "I don't want to think badly of her, either."

"There has to be another explanation. She's over at the tree lot now." He shook his head. "You've seen how hard up she's been since she returned to town. How hard she's worked to make money to support her baby. A person with this kind of hidden stash doesn't agonize over the cost of diapers."

"Unless she's been lying to everyone from the beginning. That all this—" Zach motioned "—has been a deliberate smokescreen to cover up her crime until she could disappear off the radar for good."

His mouth twisted. "Lying to me, my family, the whole town? She's not that good of an actress. I would've picked up on something. I would've—"

"Would you?"

His gut knotted. Was Zach right? Had his feelings blinded him to her real character? Images bombarded his mind. Shayla rocking Jeremiah at Thanksgiving. Hot chocolate in front of the fire. Her face when she sang the cradle lullaby at the Advent service.

Luke blew out a breath. "I'm telling you, she's innocent of wrongdoing, Zach. She hates the life her family has chosen. She'd never do anything to jeopardize Jeremiah's future."

Zach studied him until Luke grew uncomfortable under his scrutiny. "You've got it bad for her, man. Go talk to her. Hear what she has to say."

He turned.

Zach caught his arm. "But if I don't hear from you within the hour, I'm calling Chief Hollingsworth myself."

"Thank you, Zach. You won't regret giving Shayla a chance to explain."

Zach's brow furrowed. "I only hope you don't regret it."

As Luke exited the shop, he found himself thinking, praying, for the same thing.

He hoped Shayla didn't give him cause to regret it, either.

Across the square, Shayla watched Luke make his way across the green, headed toward the lot. He was scowling. Something had happened at Zach's auto shop.

The car. The cash. The pieces fell into place.

Wall had hidden the money in plain sight. The old car he kept locked in the shed behind his house in Greensboro. Images raced through her mind of all the months she'd planned her escape.

The car hidden away in a shed. The decrepit automobile he never drove. The vehicle she'd secretly restored to working order.

Her getaway to Truelove last spring. The newspaper photo after the tornado blowing her location. The final months of her pregnancy in the maternity home in Durham.

She'd done everything she could to hide, to get away, and it was all to no avail.

How had it come to this?

She rose off the front stoop of the camper when Luke neared. "You found it?"

His step faltered. His warm brown eyes went cold. His expression went hard. His wonderful rugged face that only last night had looked at her with such… She gulped past the sudden boulder in her throat.

"You knew about the money?" he rasped. "I told Zach it couldn't be true. That you wouldn't—"

"I didn't know until a few moments ago when Wall showed up."

Luke whipped around. "Jeremiah's father was here?"

"He's not Jeremiah's father." She clutched her arms around herself. "Not in any way that counts."

Luke's mouth thinned. "Blood counts."

Wincing, she lowered her eyes to the ground.

"How long have you and Wall—"

Shayla's head snapped up. "There is no Wall and me. I haven't seen him since I ran away from him. From that life. I told you I never wanted to see him again. He went to prison. But his fancy lawyer got him out on a technicality and…and…"

"And you ran. Is that what you're aiming to do now, Shayla? Run with your ill-gotten stash?" He raked his hand over his head. "Leaving the rest of us to suffer through the fallout?" He struck his chest with his clenched hand. "I defended you to Zach. What a fool I was to believe you were better than this."

He looked at her with such scorn that her heart shrank within her. This was the way the others at school used to look at her. Like she was trash. Like she was nothing.

Sudden clarity assailed her, washing away the cobwebs of doubt and fear. She was tired of running. She was sick of being the victim. She was weary of guilt by association.

No matter what it cost her—the music, the respect of friends, the love of a good man. She bit her lip to keep it from trembling.

Somehow she must gather her courage to do the right thing, to overcome the reluctance she'd been conditioned with since childhood. She was under no illusions. She'd lose everything.

They'd never believe she, a Coggins, hadn't been in on it from the beginning. Even Luke didn't believe her. Her stomach roiled.

She'd go to jail like Wall. They'd take her precious son. She might never see him again.

Her eyes stung. If only there was another way...
Stop it. Don't think like that. Don't lose your nerve.
But there was no help for it. It must be done.

Swaying, she clutched the iron railing. "Call the police chief."

Luke took a step back. She'd surprised him. "You want me to call Bridger?"

"This has to end now." Bile rose in her throat. "Before anyone else gets hurt. But I can't go to the station." Her eyes flitted left and right. "He's probably watching us. It would be better if the police chief comes to me." She moistened her lips. "Incognito."

He frowned. "You say that like..."

"Like I've done this before? I haven't. But funny what we pick up from our family of origin." She laughed, the sound dry and completely without mirth. "Morgans learn Christmas trees. Cogginses learn the ins and outs of the criminal justice system."

Strangely, it took her another ten minutes to convince Luke to pull out his phone and dial the police chief at home. He moved where she couldn't hear him, keeping his back to her as he talked to the chief. He clicked off and whirled around, almost as if he'd expected her to have done a disappearing act.

Her gut knotted. Probably what he wished. That she'd disappear from his life for good. Fifteen minutes later, the police chief pulled up beside the lot in his personal vehicle.

When the chief got out of his truck, Shayla was glad to note he was wearing jeans, brogan work boots and a heavy, fleece-lined flannel coat. Flicking her a look, the chief nodded to Luke and then nonchalantly strolled toward the stand of trees.

Bridger Hollingsworth was an imposing man in his early thirties. Tall. Black hair and piercing blue eyes. She forced her feet to move toward him. For a moment, she just stood beside him, letting him examine the tree from every angle like any normal Christmas tree buyer.

Somehow she got the impression nothing much escaped his notice. Cautious. Wary. Careful.

His gaze was never still. Scoping out potential sources of danger. She recognized the look. It belonged not only to the hunter but the hunted, as well.

"Tell me about the money," he rasped in his gravelly, authoritative tone.

She and the police chief continued to circle the tree. She told him everything she knew about Wall, and more that she suspected.

He pulled a medium-size tree from the stand. "I'll take this one. Walk with me to pay. I'll tell you what I know while Luke runs it through the baler."

Chief Hollingsworth handed the tree over to Luke and pulled her a short distance away.

"I received a call from some friends of mine last week to be on the lookout for a suspect by the name of Wall Phillips on their radar. They believed he was headed my way." The police chief arched his brow. "Federal law enforcement friends of mine."

She knotted her hands. "I didn't know about the money in the car."

"I believe you." Hooking his thumbs through his belt loops, Hollingsworth widened his stance. "You've got a devoted advocate in Luke Morgan. He presented at least a dozen arguments as to why you were an innocent bystander in this."

Luke believed her after all?

"Not to mention a fan club consisting of my wife, Maggie's great-aunt GeorgeAnne and my mother, Wilda. Whose lives you helped save, along with my boys last spring during the tornado." The hard line of his mouth softened. "And I heard you sing last night."

Her hand went to her throat.

"I make it my business to ask around about newcomers to our peaceful little town. Including the new waitress at the Mason Jar Café." He shrugged. "Occupational hazard. Before I headed over here, I also put in a call to my friends at the Asheville office."

She tensed. "The FBI?"

"They'll be here in about an hour. They've been trying to nail Wall Phillips for years. For money laundering. Racketeering. And obstruction of justice in an ongoing, parallel investigation involving a couple of his associates." The Truelove police chief made a face. "Drug traffickers."

"Wall launders their money."

Hollingsworth pursed his lips. "He's their front man. The legitimate public face on their not-so-legal enterprise. And now he's under pressure from his partners in crime to produce their laundered profits. They'll kill him if he doesn't. And soon."

She took a deep breath. "I didn't know about his business dealings until I'd already gotten involved with him. And then I was trapped. He—he threatened me."

The police chief's eyes bored into her. "He was physically abusive?"

She looked away. "People always ask why I didn't leave sooner, but I was afraid of him and what he would do. He had me convinced I deserved his treatment, and no one would help me."

"Abusers manipulate and isolate."

She lifted her chin. "When he was arrested and I found out I was pregnant, I knew I had to get away for my baby's sake."

"The federal agents are headed to the Mason Jar. I told them to come mountain casual so as not to arouse suspicion. I'm going to put the tree in my truck and head over there, as well."

Luke rejoined them and handed the police chief the bundled evergreen.

Hollingsworth hefted the tree. "Give it sixty minutes, then I want you to take a coffee break, too, Shayla. They'll want to hear everything again."

Luke straightened. "I'll come with her."

The chief flicked him a look. "Too suspicious if no one is manning the tree lot." Luke opened his mouth to protest, but Hollingsworth held up his hand. "Let law enforcement do their job, Luke."

A mutinous look in his eyes, Luke clamped his jaw tight.

"Wall threatened Jeremiah." She was so ashamed she could hardly get the next words from her lips. "Luke's family, too."

The chief nodded. "I'll send an officer out to the farm."

"Wall mustn't be allowed to get his hands on my son. He'll use Jeremiah as a bargaining chip." She seized Luke's arm. "Promise me, no matter what happens, you won't let him take my baby."

Luke frowned. "Nothing is going to happen to him."

Tears filled her eyes. "I can do this only so long as I know you'll make sure Jeremiah is okay. If you ever felt anything for me as a friend…"

He jerked. "A friend?"

"Promise me, Luke," she pleaded. "Please."

A light dimmed in his gaze. The light she'd glimpsed whenever he looked at her had been extinguished by her unsavory past.

"I'd never let anything happen to the boy." He scowled. "I'd hoped you knew me better than that." He stalked toward the camper.

For a split second, she closed her eyes. Her father had warned her. This was what she did. She ruined people.

Maybe it was for the best she'd no longer be in Luke's life. She was doing the right thing.

But, oh, how doing the right thing hurt.

Chapter Fourteen

The plan put forward by the federal agents was easy in its simplicity. Too easy.

Just after noon, Luke stomped around the tree lot, loading the last of the unsold trees into his truck. Shayla was still closeted in Kara's office at the café with the agents.

Bridger hadn't left him entirely out of the loop. The police chief called, letting him know the decisions that had been made. To maintain her cover, he was supposed to pick up Shayla at the café and take her home until the rendezvous at midnight with Phillips.

The agents were setting a trap for Wall to incriminate himself. Eager to make amends, Shayla had readily agreed to participate in bringing him to justice. She'd wear a wireless recording device and get him to confess on tape to his crimes.

But suppose Wall discovered the transmitter? What then?

Luke unplugged the snowman, which deflated quickly. Kind of like how his heart was feeling. He couldn't shake the sense of unease he felt at the idea of Shayla putting herself in harm's way.

There were too many variables out of law enforcement's control. Too much could go wrong. And where would that leave Shayla?

He didn't know the federal guys, but he understood enough to know their real interest was in capturing Phillips. They weren't concerned for her welfare. Or if they were, it extended only as far as she could help them in apprehending Phillips.

Luke locked the camper and surveyed the empty lot. Between Christmas and New Year, he'd return to dismantle the light strings and remove the poles.

Who was looking out for Shayla? His heart constricted. Who had ever looked out for her? No one, that's who.

There were so many ways this operation could go sideways. His head pounded. Wall Phillips was a dangerous, evil man.

A man who'd mistreat a woman and profit from human frailty was capable of anything. He'd never felt such anger before.

Not at Shayla, but at those who over the years had told her lies about herself. Making her believe she deserved no better than someone like Wall

Phillips. Her mother's abandonment. Her father's neglect, abuse of another stripe. They were both to blame.

As he thought about how the smooth-talking criminal had terrorized her, he clenched and unclenched his fists. If he could get his hands on that jerk for five minutes…

His chest heaving and his jaw tight, he strode toward the truck and yanked open the door. He didn't care what Bridger or the FBI said. He would have Shayla's back if no one else would.

The world needed her beautiful voice. Jeremiah needed his mother. Luke scrubbed his hand over his face. And even if she would never be a part of his life, he would do what he had to do to make sure she got to live out her dreams.

The ride to the farm in Luke's truck was even more quiet than the ride to town. His gaze fixed on the road ahead, he kept his thoughts to himself.

But Shayla could well imagine what he thought of her and the trouble she'd inadvertently brought down on his family.

Krista peered out the front door. "Why is Officer Thomas sitting in the driveway?"

"Where's Jeremiah?" Shayla whispered.

Emily motioned upstairs. "We put him down for his afternoon nap."

Desperate to reassure herself her child was safe,

she took the stairs two at a time. Leaving Luke to explain to his family what a mess she'd made of not only Christmas, but their lives, too.

She slipped into the darkened bedroom. Tiptoeing across the rug, she sank onto the edge of the bed and drank her fill of her tiny son sleeping peacefully in the crib. She memorized the fluttery curve of his lashes and imprinted the dimple in his cheek into her mind.

Once Wall was arrested, she would become one of the prosecution's chief witnesses at the trial. Her life, her hopes, her dreams would be forever changed.

This Christmas had been nothing but a peaceful interlude in the storm of her life, but she'd look back on her time at the farm with gratitude. A lovely, if fleeting, dream she would cherish forever.

She spent the rest of the afternoon cuddling her son, savoring every moment. Not knowing once she left to make the transfer if she'd ever see him again.

Through tears, Emily and the girls promised her they would watch over him. She'd expected resentment if not outright anger from Luke's family, but there was none of that. Only hugs and assurances of their love. That stunned her, since she'd managed to put their lives in jeopardy, too.

She gazed at her baby, cradled in her arms.

They were the family she'd always wanted. However, Luke made his feelings only too clear. He'd spent the afternoon in the barn, avoiding her like the plague, only appearing briefly at dinner. His face was like a thundercloud.

And on the off chance she hadn't gotten the drift of his feelings, he excused himself after dinner for a guys' night out with his buddies at the firehouse. She might never see him again, and he hadn't bothered to wish her well, much less say goodbye.

The door clicked shut behind him. It was all she could do to keep from bursting into tears. Emily reached for her hand. Caroline reached for the other.

"We're going to pray while you're gone. For God's purposes to be accomplished. For a peaceful resolution to this—this—"

"I think the word you're looking for is *disaster*," she choked. "I'm so, so sorry." She bit back a sob. "For everything."

Krista wound her arms around Shayla. "We'll never be sorry you came into our lives. We love you, Shayla." The younger girl wept on her shoulder.

Shayla felt like weeping, but she dared not. If she did, she'd never stop. Luke hadn't even stuck around to pray. He must hate her so much to have put his family in danger.

Even if he didn't feel for her the same as she felt

for him, she'd believed he was her friend. *You are so stupid, Shayla. So pathetic.*

Later, she held her son close to her heart one last time before she put him down for the night. Standing beside his crib, she inhaled the sweet baby scent of him.

She kissed his chubby baby fingers one by one. Loving him with every fiber of her being. Trying to convince herself he'd be better off without her in his life.

The federal agents arrived around ten o'clock for a final briefing. That afternoon they'd inventoried and supervised the removal of the cash from the car in Zach's garage. Chief Hollingsworth would bring it with him as the rendezvous with Wall drew closer.

Caroline helped her conceal the wireless transmitter behind the top button of her winter coat. The agents left to take up their positions in an unmarked van parked down the block from the gazebo on the square. They'd be listening, recording and monitoring her entire exchange with Wall. When the transaction was complete, they would swoop in and arrest him.

Dry-eyed, Shayla sat on the couch, Caroline and Emily on either side, their arms around her. Utterly spent, she was beyond the need for tears now. Krista kept watch out the front window for the Truelove police chief.

Shayla would drive Emily's SUV into town. Bridger would accompany her, concealed in the floor of the back seat but close at hand should she require more immediate backup.

There was a crunch of tires on the gravel in the driveway. A car door slammed. From the front porch, Bridger's deep voice checked in with the officer on duty. Krista had the door open before the police chief could knock.

His shrewd, discerning glance took in the entire room as well as its occupants in a single glance. "It's time." He handed Shayla the black duffel bag she guessed contained the cash.

Krista broke into tears. Caroline went to her sister. Emily gave Shayla one last hug. Her throat tight, she followed the police chief out to the SUV.

She slipped behind the wheel. The police chief folded his linebacker frame into the narrow confines of the back seat. Gripping the wheel, she stared blankly into the darkness of the night.

"Are you ready, Shayla?"

She started the motor. "Ready as I'll ever be."

The ride to town had never felt so brief and, at the same time, so long. She kept her attention trained on the winding yellow ribbon of the curving mountain road.

On the outskirts of town, she drove past the welcome sign to Truelove—Where True Love

Awaits. Because of her past, she'd singlehandedly destroyed any chance of that happening for herself.

Perhaps she was never meant to know real love. But she prayed that someday Luke would. He'd make someone a wonderful husband. Just not for her.

The SUV clattered over the bridge. Nearly midnight, Main Street was deserted. Trying not to be obvious, she scoped out the block. But the federal agents were good at their jobs. The operations van wasn't anywhere to be seen.

All of Truelove slept. The businesses were shuttered. Not a single light shone from the homes in the surrounding neighborhoods.

In the crisp chill of the December air, stars glimmered vividly against the inky blackness of the night sky. Only the lighted snowflakes attached to the utility poles cast a festive glow upon the sidewalks. She pulled the car alongside the curb at the café and parked.

"I'll be close, Shayla, and I'll be praying for you," the police chief whispered from behind her seat.

"Thank you," she rasped.

She grabbed the duffel strap and eased out of the SUV. Shaking, she walked down the sidewalk and entered the square through the row of newly planted saplings.

It was darker in the middle of the green where

the gleam of the streetlights did not penetrate. Something scurried on the snowy ground near her foot. Going stock-still, she almost screamed.

A brisk wind off the mountain set the treetops of the surviving oaks rustling. Reaching up to the sky, the winter-bare branches scraped against one another and grated on her already unsettled nerves.

Taking a second to let her heart settle, she reminded herself to breathe. She was almost to the gazebo. The painted white structure loomed out of the darkness ahead of her.

No sign of Wall. Maybe he wouldn't show up. Maybe—

Somewhere not too distant, a hoot owl screeched and she nearly jumped out of her skin. But just as quickly, she steeled herself.

As she reached the steps, a shadow emerged from the recesses of the night. "Do you have my money?"

She removed the strap from her shoulder. "It's a lot of money."

He towered over her. "Show me."

The agents had coached her into how to draw him into a confession. Sitting the bag on the step, she unzipped the duffel. Shouldering her aside, Wall dug into the contents. He pulled out a stack of bills and rifled through them.

"It's all there, Wall. I wouldn't try to cheat you."

"'Cause you know what would happen if you did," he huffed, continuing to comb through the duffel.

"So much money, Wall." She injected a note of flattery in her voice. He liked nothing so much as to feel powerful and blindly adored. "I can't tell you how impressed I am."

Not a lie. Self-preservation prevented her from telling him what she really thought of him. The truth would earn her a punch to the gut or worse.

"Where did it come from?" She kept her gaze lowered to the ground. Dealing with Wall was like dealing with a feral creature. Direct eye contact often prompted aggression. "Is—is it all yours?"

She layered her words with uncertain hesitation. Best to allow him to believe he was in control. Do nothing to challenge him until he'd incriminated himself.

He zipped the bag shut. "I invest money for my clients. They expect a return on their investment." He sneered at her. "Not something someone with your lack of smarts can grasp, but you taking off with their money has put me in an uncomfortable situation."

"I'm sorry, Wall."

She wasn't sorry, but it seemed the prudent thing to say.

"Do you have any idea how much trouble you've

caused me?" His eyes glittered. "These are not the kind of people you want unhappy."

She inched back a step. A precautionary measure. Out of striking distance. In case he was winding up to take out his displeasure on her. "I didn't realize you'd stashed anything inside the vehicle."

He took a step forward. "But you knew the car wasn't yours." Somehow, he'd gotten between her and escape.

Shayla's breath hitched. *Think fast. Don't let him see the fear.*

"It's like you always say, though. To the victor belong the spoils." She forced herself to touch the sleeve of his leather jacket and prayed he didn't notice how her hand shook. "Such a lot of money you were so clever to earn for them. Some of it surely must belong to you."

He chuckled. "I was clever. Very clever." Then he proceeded, because he couldn't resist the opportunity to brag, to tell her how he'd made his clients so much money. And he made the mistake of naming them.

Gotcha. Not as clever as he believed himself to be; but nor was she as dumb as he thought her.

She started to ease around him. "All's well that ends—"

"Where do you think you're going?"

Her gaze darted left and right. Where were the agents? Surely they had enough to charge him.

Looming over her, he shoved her against the foundation of the gazebo. She winced as splinters of wood dug into her shoulder blades. Where was Chief Hollingsworth? The agents?

Trapped, her chest heaved in an effort not to give in to the panic. Cajole. Flatter. Divert. "Please don't be mad, Wall."

Wall got in her face. "I don't get mad." His lip curled. "I get even."

He grabbed her throat. She cried out. She couldn't breathe.

And then something—someone—flew out of the shadows, wrenching Wall's hand from around her neck and knocking her tormentor to the ground.

Doors slammed. Shouts rang out from every corner of the square. Snow crunched beneath running feet. Bridger. The federal agents.

She gasped, trying to fill her lungs with air. Zach. Sam Gibson? She caught a brief glimpse of a navy blue uniform of the Truelove Fire Department. What were the firefighters doing here?

And Luke. He'd come. He hadn't left her to face this alone.

The men rolled on the ground, but Wall managed to free himself and jumped to his feet. He pulled a gun from the back of his waistband and pointed it at Luke.

Staring up the barrel of the gun, Luke froze.

"Come any closer," Wall yelled, "and I'll kill him."

All movement immediately came to a standstill.

She had to save Luke. He and Jeremiah were the only good things in her life. Wall Phillips had taken so much from her.

Her self-respect. Her confidence. Her trust.

She wasn't going to allow him to harm anyone else. Certainly not the man she loved. She was done playing the victim. She'd had it with men like him who thought it their right to terrorize.

No more. The abuse stopped here. Tonight.

She yanked one of the plastic candy canes framing the gazebo steps out of the ground. He never saw it coming. She knocked him upside the head with the candy cane.

Not enough to bring him down but enough to shift him off his feet. He staggered.

Taken by surprise, he lost his grip on the gun. It fell with a thud into the snow. The blow wasn't much, but it allowed Luke to regain the upper hand.

Springing forward like a coiled tiger, he brought Wall Phillips to his knees.

It took Bridger and one of the federal agents to haul him off Wall. The other agent clapped

Wall into handcuffs and dragged him to his feet. Fists curled, the not-so-stoic-now Christmas tree farmer surged forward and would have tackled Wall again, except Zach forcibly held him back. Actually, it took both Sam and Zach to hold Luke back.

Spent, she sank onto the gazebo steps. Shocked and shaken. Truelove police officers were suddenly everywhere. Could the night get any more bizarre? Miss GeorgeAnne's Walter, the retired judge, appeared to be arguing with one of the agents.

GeorgeAnne plopped down on the step beside her.

"What're you doing here, Miss GeorgeAnne?" Her eyes widened at the crowbar in the older lady's hand. "And what were you planning on doing with that?"

GeorgeAnne's mouth thinned. "Whatever I had to do. Truelove protects its own." Wrapping her bony arm around Shayla, she gave her a hard, fierce hug.

Miss GeorgeAnne considered her one of Truelove's own? Like she truly belonged here?

"What took you so long?" Fire Chief Will MacKenzie yelled at his best friend, Bridger.

"There was a glitch with the electronics. Delayed our response." Police Chief Bridger Hollingsworth jabbed his finger in the air. "But you and your smoke eaters have got no call to be here. You're interfering in police business."

"What concerns Luke Morgan is my business," Kara's husband growled. "Which makes Shayla practically a part of the fire department family. My guys formed a perimeter around the green to make sure your *lot*—" he snarled "—didn't let him get away."

Bridger's face turned an unhealthy shade of red. "I ought to charge all of you," he said, his hand sweeping toward the grumbling circle of firefighters. "With obstruction of justice."

"Stop squabbling this instant!" GeorgeAnne waved an imperious hand. "Don't make me call ErmaJean and IdaLee to come down here. You know the night air is not good for ErmaJean's lungs."

The men exchanged sheepish looks.

Bridger let loose a low laugh. "I've lived here long enough to know better than to cross them."

Will chuckled. "Only in Truelove, right?"

The men moved away to deal with the unfolding situation together.

GeorgeAnne's mouth twitched. "I've retained my gentleman friend, Walter, to represent you in this matter, Shayla."

"But, Miss—"

"You can thank me later." The older woman lifted her hand, palm out. "Walter may be a retired judge, but he never let his license to practice law lapse. Top-notch defense attorney in his day. Never lost a case. Like a shark, he can't wait to sink his teeth into another challenging case."

Walter strolled over to them. "That was fun." He grinned. "Phillips is spilling his guts, eager to make a deal and turn state's evidence against the drug cartel."

Her heart sank. "So they're letting him go?"

"Not at all." Walter offered her his hand. "The government's offer is for protection and better conditions in the federal penitentiary where he will spend a great number of years."

Taking his hand, she rose. "I guess the agents will be over here soon to take me into custody."

Walter squeezed her hand. "No charges are being filed against you. I made sure of it."

"Didn't I tell you?" GeorgeAnne grinned at him. "Walter's got a killer instinct."

A lump formed in her throat. "Oh, Mr. . . ." She didn't know his last name. "Mr. Walter, thank you." She angled toward the matchmaker. "As soon as I get some money, I'll repay the retainer, Miss GeorgeAnne. And Walter's fee."

GeorgeAnne harrumphed. "The retainer was one dollar."

Walter's silver hair gleamed in the moonlight. "A copy of your first record album will be payment enough for me."

GeorgeAnne frowned. "I don't think the music industry does record albums anymore, Walt."

"I thought I heard records were making a comeback." He took her arm in his. "This is why I need you, Georgie. To keep me current."

Shayla folded her arms around herself. "But what about the trial?"

Walter smiled. "With Phillips falling over himself to save his own skin, your testimony will not be needed. You're free to go home." He slipped GeorgeAnne's arm through the crook of his elbow.

Home?

She wasn't sure where that was, but she knew where she wanted home to be—with Luke. She'd only needed to listen to her heart, as IdaLee said. And her heart was saying she should stay. In Truelove. With Luke.

But did he still want her? After all the trouble she'd brought him? Yet surely he must have some feeling for her to have saved her from Wall.

She looked for him and didn't see him anywhere on the square. Had he left already? Without her? Panicked, she ran out of the square and onto the street.

His truck was parked behind the SUV on Main. He straightened when she approached. "Bridger told me about the fed's deal with Phillips. That you won't be needed to testify."

Luke hadn't left her. He'd waited. Her heart felt

giddy with relief and joy. Happiness bubbled up inside her.

"I'm free," she rasped. "I think the feeling is only now beginning to sink in."

Why was he just standing there? But most people would find it hard to understand the shadow her past had cast over her life unless they'd lived it. She'd simply have to make him understand.

"I'm free of Wall. Free of my family. Free to follow my heart." She threw her arms around him.

He stiffened.

Reaching up behind him, he removed her hands from around his neck. "You're free to follow your heart to Nashville."

She swallowed. "You think I should go to Nashville? I thought—"

"You have a gift, Shayla. And it would be wasted here in Truelove." He scrubbed his hand over his face. "Wasted on a Christmas tree farmer like me."

Her heart lay as heavy in her chest as a boulder. "You want Jeremiah and I to go."

"Tonight didn't change anything that matters."

"B-but you...me..." Her voice went small. "I'd hoped—"

"You have a great future ahead of you, Shayla." His Adam's apple bobbed in his throat. "One day, I'll hear you on the radio and remember when we were friends."

Friends. Was that all she was to him?

Suddenly it became very important he not see her cry. The tears she'd held at bay the entire evening had caught up with her, threatening to burst forth from behind her fragile grip on self-control.

If she didn't get away from him right then and there, she was going to disgrace herself. He didn't deserve to have to carry the guilt of unrequited feelings. It wasn't his fault he didn't feel for her as she felt for him.

He'd been nothing but good and kind to her. Her hero at least three times over. The best friend she'd ever had.

With effort she pulled her shattered emotions together. "Jeremiah and I can leave on the first bus tomorrow."

The warmth she so loved faded from his eyes. His face, every line dear to her, had become unreadable. Remote. Mr. Stoic. "The day before Christmas Eve?"

"No reason to stay." She searched his features. "Is there?"

"I guess not." Refusing to meet her gaze, he pushed off from the SUV. "I'll follow you to the farm."

She managed to drive to the farmhouse without mishap. Emily, Caroline and Krista met her at the door. Dropped off earlier by another officer to retrieve his personal vehicle, Bridger had already explained how the situation had been resolved.

Luke's family engulfed her in hugs, but she remained oddly detached. Emotionless. Almost as if she were outside on the porch, looking in on this version of herself and the Morgan family.

The family that was never going to be hers. And Luke, standing off to the side, perhaps feeling as detached from everything as she did.

In that moment, she totally got the barricades he placed around his heart. Envied him that, even. This was why it was better not to depend upon anyone.

The wrench of parting was simply too great to be borne. She should have never allowed herself to get so attached to the Morgans. And most especially, not Luke.

She told them of her plan to leave the next morning. His family protested. There were more tears. Luke remained as silent as the grave.

She was so exhausted she could no longer think straight as she said her goodbyes. Then, because she could bear the ache inside her no more, she went upstairs to her son.

Once she closed the door behind her, she gave in to the sobs building inside her chest. She curled into a ball and lay on the bed. For fear of waking her baby, she stuffed her fist in her mouth to muffle the sounds. She wept for herself and for Luke.

But mostly for the love neither one of them would ever know with each other.

Chapter Fifteen

~~❧~~

The next morning at the bus terminal, Luke waited for the announcement that would begin Shayla's journey far away from everyone who loved her.

Did he love her? He couldn't bring himself to admit it to himself, yet he remained sick inside at the idea of never seeing her again. Never holding her again. Never being part of her life again.

But it was for the best. *Isn't it, God?* He refused to hold her back from fully claiming her gift.

Overhead, the intercom crackled. "Calling all passengers headed to Nashville…"

He jerked.

"At this time, passengers, please proceed with your luggage to the bus for departure."

They both rose. For one too-brief moment, he held tightly to Jeremiah. One final hug. He brushed his lips across Jeremiah's forehead. Relishing the sweet scent of baby shampoo.

With great reluctance, he returned the little boy to his car seat and snapped the safety straps in place. His stomach churned. "I'll walk you to the bus."

Her lips thinned. "You really don't have to do that." She'd been aloof with him all morning. Remote. Her usually expressive features were unreadable.

And he missed her. She was standing here beside him still, but he already missed her—he missed them—so much he was afraid his heart was going to short-circuit from the sheer amount of pain he was feeling.

"I want to walk you to the bus, Shayla." His nostrils flared. "Besides, how would you manage to carry the car seat and two suitcases?"

She took hold of the car seat. "I'd find a way. I always do."

He hefted the suitcases, one in each hand.

"Thank you." She swallowed. "For everything. I'm leaving with far more than I arrived with."

His mother and the girls had insisted she take the gifts already under the tree for her and Jeremiah. Luke had bought her a prepaid cell phone.

Luke shook his head. "I should be thanking you. From day one, you stepped up to do whatever needed doing."

Gripping the car seat, she followed the crowd

surging through the double doors to the departure terminal outside.

He followed with the suitcases. "I don't know how we would have made it through the season without your help. And when I think about how close we came to losing the farm and now how things have turned around—"

"As a result of your hard work and God's blessing."

Passengers milled around, waiting their turn to board.

He set the suitcases down on the sidewalk to be loaded underneath the bus. "You and Jeremiah have been God's blessing. To my family. To me. Without your support—"

"Luke Morgan?" The bus driver poked the brim of his cap higher on his forehead. "It *is* you." He held out his hand. "Victor Burns."

"One of our most faithful customers." Luke nodded. "You've been buying choose-and-cut trees from us for years."

"It doesn't feel like Christmas until we get our tree from the Morgans."

Luke turned toward her. "Shayla and her son, Jeremiah, are headed to Nashville with you today."

"Glad to have you aboard, ma'am. And what about you, Luke?" The older man grinned. "Leaving the farm for Christmas?"

"He's not coming." She nudged the black suitcase with her boot. "The farm is his life."

Luke winced.

"I better get back to work. We've got a schedule to keep." The driver shoved the suitcases under the bus. "Merry Christmas to you." Tipping his hat, he moved to help another passenger.

Luke folded his arms across his chest. "I guess this is goodbye, then."

She tucked a strand of hair behind her ear. "I guess it is." Carrying Jeremiah in the car seat, she took a step toward the waiting line.

His insides clenched. "Shayla?"

She stopped. "Yes?" Her face tilted toward him, reflecting the same hope and longing he felt with every fiber of his being.

"Nothing."

Her face fell.

"It's best this way."

Her mouth trembled. "If you say so."

Luke's arms fell to his side. "I hope all of your dreams come true."

She glanced at the open door of the waiting bus. "No one's dreams all come true."

He laid his hand on Jeremiah's head. The little boy gave him a toothless grin, reaching out his arms to Luke. Stabbing him in the heart. The child he'd begun to dream could become his son. The family he and Shayla would create together.

But there was no together for them. He'd never stand in the way of her dreams. Sometimes one dream come true meant none of the others could.

She lifted her chin. "I'll never forget this Christmas."

Neither would he. "Have yourself a good life, Shayla Coggins," he rasped, barely holding it together.

Her eyes blazed with emotion. "I wish you the happiest and best of lives, Luke Morgan."

Which was impossible, of course. Because neither she nor Jeremiah would be in it. But he didn't say that out loud. He couldn't. Not if he didn't want to completely lose it in front of the bus passengers and make a spectacle of himself.

Because despite whatever else he lost, he must maintain his dignity at all costs. Mustn't he?

She reached the door of the bus, and there was no more time. Adjusting the diaper bag on her shoulder, she stepped onto the bus and he stepped away.

Through the windows on the side of the bus, he watched as she lumbered down the aisle toward her assigned row with Jeremiah. He was glad Mom had convinced her to spend the extra money to get the additional ticket for the car seat. Both she and Jeremiah would rest more comfortably during the trip with their own seats. He would have to ride rear-facing but would be content as long as he could see Shayla's face.

She slipped the diaper bag off her shoulder and settled her son in the adjoining seat. After she latched the car seat in place, she sat down.

He lifted his hand to wave, but she stared out the opposite side of the bus. His gut clenched. He let his hand drop. But it was for the best.

Best she forget about him. Jeremiah would never remember this first Christmas. And the idea pricked Luke's heart more than it reasonably should. Best he forgot about them, too.

Easier said than done.

Victor Burns boarded the bus last. With a whooshing hiss, he closed the doors. The bus pulled away from the curb. And soon it disappeared from his sight.

Hunching his shoulders against the cold, he retraced his steps to his truck in the parking lot. He threw himself into the cab and fisted his hands around the steering wheel. His head throbbed. His heart ached.

The farm is his life. The farm is his life. The farm is his life...

He flinched.

The farm is his life?

He stared bleakly out the windshield. The farm was *not* his life. The farm had been his family's home for generations.

But his mother and sisters were making a new life for themselves, a new home. Shayla and Jeremiah had become home for him. What good was the farm to him if the home of his heart was leaving him?

God, forgive me for not seeing what was in front of my face all along. The gifts You gave me. To cherish. To nurture. To love.

Shayla Coggins was the love of his life. And Jeremiah was the son of his heart. He rested his forehead against the cold leather of the wheel. How could he have been so blind? So stubborn?

His head snapped up. *Dear God, have I lost them forever? Show me what to do. How do I fix this?*

As quietly as a gentle wind, an idea whispered through his mind.

For the first time in his life, he understood that true love required sacrifice.

Yet, after everything she'd endured, could Shayla love him? Was it possible for her to trust someone as unworthy of her love as him?

He set his jaw and prayed to be the kind of man she could trust. The sort of man to whom she could securely give her heart. He prayed to be worthy of the treasure of a woman like Shayla Coggins.

Luke's eyes darted to the dashboard clock, afraid he was already too late. He palmed the wheel. God had brought them both too far to turn back now.

And no matter what he had to do, he would make this right.

Tired from the effort of not dissolving into tears, Shayla stared straight ahead over the seat in front of her at the back of some nameless, faceless passenger's head. Willing herself not to cry.

The bus rumbled down the block.

He didn't want her. Who would? So much baggage. Such an embarrassment. He and his family were well rid of her.

What had she expected? A silly, romantic moment? Had she actually envisioned a scenario where Mr. Stoic brought the bus to a standstill and, amid the curious glances of onlookers, declared his undying love?

How stupid, hopeless and naive could she be? That sort of thing only happened in movies. Or to someone like the glamorous AnnaBeth. Never to her.

Would she never learn? Cogginses didn't get happily-ever—

Just then, the bus driver slammed on the brakes. She and the other passengers lurched forward in their seats. Instinctively she put out an arm to protect Jeremiah, but his car seat was safely strapped in beside her.

"Sorry, folks," Victor Burns called. "There's a truck blocking the road."

A truck? She frowned. Around her, people murmured, pointing toward the front of the bus.

"Shayla!" Victor yelled. "You've got a visitor."

Releasing her seat belt with a quick snap, she rose out of her seat. What was going on?

There was a hiss as the driver opened the bus doors. Luke appeared at the end of the aisle. Her breath hitched.

Catching sight of her, his face lifted. He strode down the aisle toward her. "Pardon me. Excuse me." Nodding his head at the other passengers, he said, "Sorry for the delay. I promise to get y'all on the road again ASAP."

She scowled. "What are you doing here?"

Everyone turned in their seats, giving her and Luke their rapt attention. She flushed.

"I forgot to tell you something."

"You blocked the road and stopped the bus to tell me something?" She propped her hands on her hips. "Ever think of texting? Emailing? Or calling me?" Her voice rose.

He folded his arms across his coat. "It needed to be said in person."

Jeremiah made cooing noises. Unfolding, Luke's face softened. Her gaze cut to her son, wriggling in his car seat.

Luke eased forward. "Hey, little buddy."

Grunting, Jeremiah stretched out his arms.

She stepped in front of her son. "I don't know what you think you're doing. Or what you want from me, but you're making a spectacle—"

"I don't care if I make a spectacle of myself." He threw his arms wide. "In fact, I feel like shouting so everyone in the world can hear."

Her eyes flicked from him to the surrounding passengers. "Have you lost your mind?" she hissed.

"The opposite. I'm finally in my right mind." He took a breath. "I love you."

She stared at him. "You what?"

His eyes bored into hers. "I love you."

"You can't love me," she whispered.

He jutted his chin. "But I do. And I don't see any reason why you and Jeremiah should have to ride to Nashville on this uncomfortable bus—" He threw a look over his shoulder. "No offense, Victor."

The bus driver threw up his hand. "None taken."

Luke faced her again. "I can just as easily drive you there myself."

Her mouth fell open. "But you can't leave the farm."

"Who says I can't?"

Her eyebrows rose. "The farm is your—"

"The farm is not my life," he growled. "And I

hope you'll forgive me for ever being so stupid to make you feel it was more important than you."

"It's kind of you to offer to drive us." This was one of the things that made her love him so much—his caring, protective nature. "But we already have our tickets. We're on the bus. We'll be fine."

"Didn't offer to be kind." He scrubbed his hand over his beard stubble. "I'm not making myself clear. What I'm trying to say is, I'm going to Nashville with you."

She frowned. "What? For how long?"

"For good. Forever. To stay." He toed the aisle with his boot. "If you and Jeremiah will have me." His gaze lifted and found hers. "I want to be your husband. I want Jeremiah to be my son. But the real question is, what do you want, Shayla? Do you want me in your life?"

Seconds ticked by, and she could only stare at him.

"For the love of sweet tea." A few rows behind her, IdaLee popped out of her seat. "Answer the boy, Shayla. He's dying inside."

Her mouth dropped open. "Miss IdaLee? What are you doing on the bus to Tennessee?"

"Eloping." The diminutive old lady threw her seat companion a fond look. "Charles proposed last night."

Leaning into the aisle, Charles waved.

Shayla exchanged a puzzled look with Luke.

"We're both too old to be driving over the mountains, so we decided to catch the bus. And save everyone the bother of a wedding. At our age, we've no time to waste."

"Let me get this straight, Miss IdaLee." She cocked her head. "You two decided, without so much as a by-your-leave, to run off together?"

"When it's real, it's real."

Charles rose to stand beside his runaway bride. He stumbled a bit, but the retired schoolteacher placed her hand gently on his arm to steady him. They smiled at each other.

A longing, sharp and sweet, rose in her chest. For a love story of her own. For something just as real. And true.

IdaLee's violet blue eyes twinkled. "I always did want a Christmas wedding. What do you say, Shayla? Do you love Luke or not?"

Her heart thundered. "I—I do."

"Don't tell me, child." IdaLee fluttered her blue-veined hand. "Tell him."

Luke reached for her. "Shayla?"

His palm, so strong and callused from hard, honest work, felt warm against her skin. As always, she felt safe with him.

"Talk to me, Shay. Tell me what you feel."

She closed her eyes. Shay. "I love you with all my heart." Her eyes flew open. "But I can't let you give up everything for me. You can't run away from your life. From your gift."

"I'm not running away." He cleared his throat. "I'm running toward you. To my future."

Jeremiah let out an exasperated cry.

She sighed. "He hears his favorite person on earth and he doesn't understand why he can't get to you."

"Can I hold him? I've missed him so much."

She laughed. "You held him in your arms not thirty minutes ago."

"Thirty minutes too long." He gave her a slow smile, the kind that made her knees go weak.

After unbuckling Jeremiah, he lifted her son into his arms. He kissed the baby's forehead and reached for her hand. "You and Jeremiah are God's gifts to me."

Her vision blurred. With her child in his arms, he fell to one knee. The entire bus gasped. Her trembling hand went to her throat.

"Will you make me the happiest man on earth and become my wife?"

"Yes." Her voice wobbled. "Oh, yes."

Letting out a whoop, he jumped to his feet. The passengers clapped and cheered.

"Here." IdaLee reached out to them. "Let me take the baby before the two of you squash him."

Luke deposited her son—their son—into the old woman's arms and took the opportunity to enfold Shayla into a tender embrace and give her a proper kiss.

After they broke apart, he grinned. "I think we'll be getting off here, Victor."

Moments later, Shayla found herself standing on the sidewalk. Despite the cold, passengers leaned out the windows, full of well wishes for a long and happy life together. Then the red taillights of the bus disappeared around the bend of the road.

Luke buckled Jeremiah into the truck cab. He deposited the suitcases in the truck bed. "Ready?"

She chewed her lip. "I think we should go back to the farm."

"No." He reared. "I've thought this through. I've got about a month before I'll be needed on the farm. Plenty of time for us to get married and set up house in Nashville while you pursue your career. I'll find someone to manage the farm in my absence."

"You love the farm, Luke. It's part of who you are."

"I do love the farm." His arms went around her as they stood next to the truck. "But not as much as I love you and Jeremiah. Not as much as I want us to be a family."

"We can be a family on the farm."

He shook his head. "I won't let you lose this chance with Oliver West. Yours is a voice the world needs to hear. A God-given talent I won' let you waste."

"Oh, my dearest darlin'." She cupped the rougl stubble of his jaw in her palm. "How I do love you for your willingness to sacrifice yourself for me but I can't let you rip yourself away from you land."

His breath fogged in the air. "I won't stand ir the way of your dreams."

"That's the beautiful thing about God-giver dreams." She nuzzled her lips across his cheek "Dreams can grow, become bigger and better by making room for other dreams, too. Your dreams And the dreams we make come true together."

His brow furrowed. "I don't know what you mean."

"Thanks to the digital world we live in, there' nothing stopping us from doing both. Songs car be written at the farm as well as in Nashville. Anc when it's time to go to the recording studio, Nash ville isn't that far away."

He lifted her hands to his lips. "Are you sure that's what you want to do?"

"I'm sure." She smiled. "We can make this work. For the farm. For my career. For us. I wan Jeremiah and our other children to have roots anc wings."

He kissed her fingers. "Other children?"

She gave him a sideways glance. "Because you're so good with babies."

"You inspire me."

She fluttered her lashes at him. "What can I say? It's a gift."

He grinned at her. "Something I have a feeling I won't ever get enough of."

She tilted her head. "And when that happens, what would you suggest I do to remedy your lack of inspiration?"

He leaned closer until only a breath separated their mouths. "Right now, a kiss would work just fine."

"A kiss?" she murmured against his lips. "If you're sure."

He ran his thumb across the apple of her cheek. "For the next sixty years, I'm sure."

She gave him a bright smile. "Well, in that case, I think something can be arranged."

And as snowflakes drifted from the sky, she did.

* * * * *

If you enjoyed this story,
check out these other Truelove stories
from author Lisa Carter

His Secret Daughter
The Twin Bargain
Stranded for the Holidays
A Mother's Homecoming
The Christmas Bargain
A Chance for the Newcomer

Find these and other great reads at
www.LoveInspired.com

Dear Reader,

The heart of this story is about embracing the gifts God has given us.

God gave us the greatest gift in His Son, Jesus Christ. He's also given each of His children at least one gift to share with others. What a privilege it is to become the hands and feet of our loving Father to someone in need.

The people He brings to us are gifts. As are the opportunities and resources He puts at our disposal. Even the pain God allows us to experience can prove to be a precious gift, growing us into His image.

How has God gifted you? How can you make an eternal difference in someone's life? I pray you will bless others with the blessings you have received.

Thank you for joining Luke, Shayla and Jeremiah on this journey of faith. I would love to hear from you at lisa@lisacarterauthor.com, or visit lisacarterauthor.com.

In His Love,
Lisa Carter

Get 4 FREE REWARDS!

We'll send you 2 FREE Books plus 2 FREE Mystery Gifts.

Love Inspired books feature uplifting stories where faith helps guide you through life's challenges and discover the promise of a new beginning.

FREE Value Over $20

YES! Please send me 2 FREE Love Inspired Romance novels and my 2 FREE mystery gifts (gifts are worth about $10 retail). After receiving them, if I don't wish to receive any more books, I can return the shipping statement marked "cancel." If I don't cancel, I will receive 6 brand-new novels every month and be billed just $5.24 each for the regular-print edition or $5.99 each for the larger-print edition in the U.S., or $5.74 each for the regular-print edition or $6.24 each for the larger-print edition in Canada. That's a savings of at least 13% off the cover price. It's quite a bargain! Shipping and handling is just 50¢ per book in the U.S. and $1.25 per book in Canada.* I understand that accepting the 2 free books and gifts places me under no obligation to buy anything. I can always return a shipment and cancel at any time. The free books and gifts are mine to keep no matter what I decide.

Choose one: ☐ **Love Inspired Romance Regular-Print** (105/305 IDN GNWC) ☐ **Love Inspired Romance Larger-Print** (122/322 IDN GNWC)

Name (please print)

Address   Apt. #

City   State/Province   Zip/Postal Code

Email: Please check this box ☐ if you would like to receive newsletters and promotional emails from Harlequin Enterprises ULC and its affiliates. You can unsubscribe anytime.

Mail to the **Harlequin Reader Service:**
IN U.S.A.: P.O. Box 1341, Buffalo, NY 14240-8531
IN CANADA: P.O. Box 603, Fort Erie, Ontario L2A 5X3

Want to try 2 free books from another series? Call 1-800-873-8635 or visit www.ReaderService.com.

*Terms and prices subject to change without notice. Prices do not include sales taxes, which will be charged (if applicable) based on your state or country of residence. Canadian residents will be charged applicable taxes. Offer not valid in Quebec. This offer is limited to one order per household. Books received may not be as shown. Not valid for current subscribers to Love Inspired Romance books. All orders subject to approval. Credit or debit balances in a customer's account(s) may be offset by any other outstanding balance owed by or to the customer. Please allow 4 to 6 weeks for delivery. Offer available while quantities last.

Your Privacy—Your information is being collected by Harlequin Enterprises ULC, operating as Harlequin Reader Service. For a complete summary of the information we collect, how we use this information and to whom it is disclosed, please visit our privacy notice located at corporate.harlequin.com/privacy-notice. From time to time we may also exchange your personal information with reputable third parties. If you wish to opt out of this sharing of your personal information, please visit readerservice.com/consumerschoice or call 1-800-873-8635. **Notice to California Residents**—Under California law, you have specific rights to control and access your data. For more information on these rights and how to exercise them, visit corporate.harlequin.com/california-privacy.   LIR21R2

Get 4 FREE REWARDS!

We'll send you 2 FREE Books plus 2 FREE Mystery Gifts.

Harlequin Heartwarming Larger-Print books will connect you to uplifting stories where the bonds of friendship, family and community unite.

FREE
Value Over
$20

YES! Please send me 2 FREE Harlequin Heartwarming Larger-Print novels and my 2 FREE mystery gifts (gifts worth about $10 retail). After receiving them, if I don't wish to receive any more books, I can return the shipping statement marked "cancel." If I don't cancel, I will receive 4 brand-new larger-print novels every month and be billed just $5.74 per book in the U.S. or $6.24 per book in Canada. That's a savings of at least 21% off the cover price. It's quite a bargain! Shipping and handling is just 50¢ per book in the U.S. and $1.25 per book in Canada.* I understand that accepting the 2 free books and gifts places me under no obligation to buy anything. I can always return a shipment and cancel at any time. The free books and gifts are mine to keep no matter what I decide.

161/361 HDN GNPZ

Name (please print)

Address   Apt. #

City   State/Province   Zip/Postal Code

Email: Please check this box ☐ if you would like to receive newsletters and promotional emails from Harlequin Enterprises ULC and its affiliates. You can unsubscribe anytime.

Mail to the **Harlequin Reader Service:**
IN U.S.A.: P.O. Box 1341, Buffalo, NY 14240-8531
IN CANADA: P.O. Box 603, Fort Erie, Ontario L2A 5X3

Want to try 2 free books from another series? Call 1-800-873-8635 or visit www.ReaderService.com.

---

*Terms and prices subject to change without notice. Prices do not include sales taxes, which will be charged (if applicable) based on your state or country of residence. Canadian residents will be charged applicable taxes. Offer not valid in Quebec. This offer is limited to one order per household. Books received may not be as shown. Not valid for current subscribers to Harlequin Heartwarming Larger-Print books. All orders subject to approval. Credit or debit balances in a customer's account(s) may be offset by any other outstanding balance owed by or to the customer. Please allow 4 to 6 weeks for delivery. Offer available while quantities last.

Your Privacy—Your information is being collected by Harlequin Enterprises ULC, operating as Harlequin Reader Service. For a complete summary of the information we collect, how we use this information and to whom it is disclosed, please visit our privacy notice located at corporate.harlequin.com/privacy-notice. From time to time we may also exchange your personal information with reputable third parties. If you wish to opt out of this sharing of your personal information, please visit readerservice.com/consumerschoice or call 1-800-873-8635. **Notice to California Residents**—Under California law, you have specific rights to control and access your data. For more information on these rights and how to exercise them, visit corporate.harlequin.com/california-privacy.

HW21R2

HARLEQUIN SELECTS COLLECTION

19 FREE BOOKS IN ALL!

NEW YORK TIMES BESTSELLING AUTHOR
RaeAnne THAYNE
A COLD CREEK HOMECOMING

LINDA LAEL MILLER
SIERRA'S HOMECOMING

DANIELS
MOUNTAIN SHERIFF

From Robyn Carr to RaeAnne Thayne to Linda Lael Miller and Sherryl Woods we promise (actually, GUARANTEE!) each author in the Harlequin Selects collection has seen their name on the *New York Times* or *USA TODAY* bestseller lists!

YES! Please send me the **Harlequin Selects Collection**. This collection begins with 3 FREE books and 2 FREE gifts in the first shipment. Along with my 3 free books, I'll also get 4 more books from the Harlequin Selects Collection, which I may either return and owe nothing or keep for the low price of $24.14 U.S./$28.82 CAN. each plus $2.99 U.S./$7.49 CAN. for shipping and handling per shipment*.If I decide to continue, I will get 6 or 7 more books (about once a month for 7 months) but will only need to pay for 4. That means 2 or 3 books in every shipment will be FREE! If I decide to keep the entire collection, I'll have paid for only 32 books because 19 were FREE! I understand that accepting the 3 free books and gifts places me under no obligation to buy anything. I can always return a shipment and cancel at any time. My free books and gifts are mine to keep no matter what I decide.

☐ 262 HCN 5576   ☐ 462 HCN 5576

Name (please print)

Address   Apt. #

City   State/Province   Zip/Postal Code

Mail to the **Harlequin Reader Service:**
IN U.S.A.: P.O. Box 1341, Buffalo, NY 14240-8531
IN CANADA: P.O. Box 603, Fort Erie, Ontario L2A 5X3

*Terms and prices subject to change without notice. Prices do not include sales taxes, which will be charged (if applicable) based on your state or country of residence. Canadian residents will be charged applicable taxes. Offer not valid in Quebec. All orders subject to approval. Credit or debit balances in a customer's account(s) may be offset by any other outstanding balance owed by or to the customer. Please allow 3 to 4 weeks for delivery. Offer available while quantities last. © 2020 Harlequin Enterprises ULC. ® and ™ are trademarks owned by Harlequin Enterprises ULC.

Your Privacy—Your information is being collected by Harlequin Enterprises ULC, operating as Harlequin Reader Service. To see how we collect and use this information visit https://corporate.harlequin.com/privacy-notice. From time to time we may also exchange your personal information with reputable third parties. If you wish to opt out of this sharing of your personal information, please visit www.readerservice.com/consumerschoice or call 1-800-873-8635. Notice to California Residents—Under California law, you have specific rights to control and access your data. For more information visit https://corporate.harlequin.com/california-privacy.

50BOOKHS22R

COMING NEXT MONTH FROM
Love Inspired

AN AMISH BABY FOR CHRISTMAS
Indiana Amish Brides • by Vannetta Chapman
In danger of losing her farm after her husband's death, pregnant widow
Abigail Yutzy needs help—even if she can't afford it. And the local bishop is
sure Amish property manager Thomas Albrecht is the perfect person to lend a
hand. But can their uneasy holiday alliance heal both their hearts?

THE AMISH OUTCAST'S HOLIDAY RETURN
by Lacy Williams
Grace Beiler knows the Amish faith demands forgiveness, but she still can't
understand why her father would offer a job and a place to stay to Zach Miller—
the man whose teenage mistake cost her sister's fiancé his life. But as she gets to
know him, even family loyalty might not be able to keep her from falling for Zach...

THE PRODIGAL'S HOLIDAY HOPE
Wyoming Ranchers • by Jill Kemerer
Hired to work on his childhood ranch at Christmas, Sawyer Roth's determined
to prove he's a changed man. The new owner's daughter, Tess Malone, will be
the hardest to convince. But as the single mom and her toddler son wriggle into
his heart, can he put the past behind him and start over?

THE PATH NOT TAKEN
Kendrick Creek • by Ruth Logan Herne
After her ex left her pregnant and alone, Devlyn McCabe never planned to tell
him about their little boy—but now Rye Bauer's back. Returning to Kendrick
Creek temporarily for his job, Rye knew he'd see Devlyn again, but he's
shocked to discover he's a father. Can the truth give them a second chance at
forever?

SNOWED IN FOR CHRISTMAS
by Gabrielle Meyer
For travel journalist Zane Harris, his little girls are his top priority. So when a
holiday snowstorm strands them with the secret mother of his eldest daughter,
he's not sure he can allow Liv Butler to bond with the child she gave up as a
teen. But Liv might just be exactly what his family needs...

CLAIMING HIS CHRISTMAS INHERITANCE
by C.J. Carroll
In her last matchmaking attempt, Zed Evans's late aunt insisted he get married
and live in the family home with his bride for three months if he wants to claim
his inheritance. So he proposes to a virtual stranger. But three holidays as
Tasha Jenkins's husband could have this confirmed bachelor wishing for a
lifetime...

**LOOK FOR THESE AND OTHER LOVE INSPIRED BOOKS WHEREVER
BOOKS ARE SOLD, INCLUDING MOST BOOKSTORES, SUPERMARKETS,
DISCOUNT STORES AND DRUGSTORES.**

LICNM1021